LAST
MAN
OUT

OTHER BOOKS OF INTEREST

From DEMERS BOOKS (www.DemersBooks.com)

Charles Merrill, *Colom: Solving the Enigma of Columbus' Origins* (October 2008). ISBN: 978-0-9816002-2-2 (paper)

Tom Graves, *Crossroads: The Life and Afterlife of Blues Legend Robert Johnson* (October 2008). ISBN: 978-0-9816002-1-5 (paper)

From MARQUETTE BOOKS (www.MarquetteBooks.com)

John W. Cones, *Dictionary of Film Finance and Distribution: A Guide for Independent Filmmakers*. ISBN 9780-922993-93-2 (cloth); 978-0-922993-94-9 (paper)

Hazel Dicken-Garcia and Giovanna Dell'Orto, Hated Ideas and the American Civil War Press (2008). ISBN 978-0-922993-89-5; 978-0-922993-88-8 (paper)

R. Thomas Berner, *Fundamentals of Journalism: Reporting, Writing and Editing* (2007). ISBN 978-0-922993-76-5 (paper)

Tomasz Pludowski (ed.), *How the World's News Media Reacted to 9/11: Essays from Around the Globe* (2007). ISBN: 978-0-922993-66-6 (paper); 978-0-922993-73-4 (cloth)

Stephen D. Cooper, *Watching the Watchdog: Bloggers as the Fifth Estate* (2006). ISBN: 0-922993-46-7 (cloth); 0-922993-47-5 (paper)

Ralph D. Berenger (ed.), *Cybermedia Go to War: Role of Convergent Media Before and During the 2003 Iraq War* (2006). ISBN: 0-922993-48-1 (cloth); 0-922993-49-1 (paper)

Jami Fullerton and Alice Kendrick, *Advertising's War on Terrorism: The Story of the Shared Values Initiative* (2006). ISBN: 0-922993-43-2 (cloth); 0-922993-44-0 (paper)

LAST
MAN
OUT

Memoirs of the Last U.S. Reporter
Castro Kicked Out of Cuba During
the Cold War

JOHN
FENTON
WHEELER

DEMERS BOOKS LLC
SPOKANE, WASHINGTON

Printed in the United States of America

CATALOGING-IN-PUBLICATION DATA

Wheeler, John Fenton, 1925-
Last man out: memoirs of the last U.S. reporter Castro
kicked out of Cuba during the Cold War / John Fenton Wheeler.
p. cm.
Includes index.
ISBN 978-0-9816002-0-8 (pbk. : alk. paper) --
1. Wheeler, John Fenton, 1925-
2. Journalists--United States--Biography.
3. Cuba--Politics and government--1959-1990.
I. Title.

2008925673

All of the photographs in this book are in the public domain.

Edited by Darcy K. Creviston

DEMERS BOOKS LLC

5915 S. Regal St., Suite 118B
Spokane, Washington 99223-6970
509-443-7057 (voice) / 509-448-2191 (fax)
books@demersbooks.com / www.DemersBooks.com

DEDICATION

To soul mate Lila, for prodding and editing;
to managing editor Jim Robertson of the
Columbia (Mo.) *Tribune,* for newspaper exposure;
to retired journalism professor John Merrill;
to family and friends who encouraged me;
and to the handful of Cuban friends I once had.

CONTENTS

PUBLISHER'S NOTE

When I worked as a newspaper reporter in Michigan in the 1970s, governmental officials often would deny me access to public records. From time to time news sources also would fail to cooperate and, in some cases, even give me false information. But until I read the draft of this book, I never realized how easy my job was.

Imagine trying to report the news in a country where the government routinely denies you access to information; where intelligence agents follow you wherever you go, deliberately trying to find (or concoct) evidence that you are a spy; and where one misstep could land you in a prison without Constitutional rights.

Those were just some of the obstacles and concerns that John Fenton Wheeler faced when he covered Cuba and Fidel Castro for the Associated Press in the late 1960s. Wheeler was the only U.S. journalist allowed to live and report in Cuba from 1967 to 1969. Castro had kicked the others out, presumably because he didn't like the stories they wrote. He allowed only one U.S. journalist to report from inside Cuba, possibly because it was easier to control that journalist.

Wheeler and his wife lived and worked in Cuba for nearly three years. Needless to say, they lived cautiously. They always assumed their phone lines and rooms were bugged and that the people they associated with were Cuban agents (many were). They avoided traveling to areas of the country or to local places that contained sensitive military or intelligence information. That surely would raise suspicions they were agents for the CIA.

However, when it came to reporting the news, Wheeler didn't cut corners. He told it like is was. Some stories made Castro and Cuba look good. Others didn't. But that kind of objectivity was never much appreciated by Castro and his government. They eventually expelled Wheeler, but not before he was able to write scores of stories about what was happening inside the Communist state — stories that no doubt helped Americans and their leaders better understand their "rogue" neighbor to the south. After Wheeler's departure in 1969, Cuba didn't allow another U.S. reporter onto its soil for more than two decades.

There are two stories in this book. One is the public story — the story of Fidel Castro and his political experiment to turn Cuba into an economic and political power. The second story is a private one — about the day-to-day lives of Wheeler and his spouse and their interactions with journalists, news-makers, politicians and others. The two stories are woven together and transport the reader back to a time when the world seemed less complicated but no less dangerous.

Last Man Out is the story of history told from the bottom up, and one that surely will peak the interest of historians, political scientists, policy makers, diplomats and political junkies for many years to come.

Contemporary map of Cuba (Courtesy of the Central Intelligence Agency)

Chapter One

IN THE LINE OF FIRE

F idel Castro was mad at somebody. I was sure it was me.

After all these years, I still remember the anxiety I felt as I watched him on television August 10, 1967, from the Associated Press office in Havana. He had been speaking for about five minutes. But I had become concerned in the first minute of his speech when he referred to "the international press." This was a Castro speech pattern — giving a few words of background to his listeners, raising his voice and setting up his next move like a baseball pitcher preparing to hurl a high hard fast ball. You don't know whether to swing or duck. I could do neither.

Some members of this international press, Castro went on, had in recent days reported "in a spirit of honest journalism; others without much journalistic honesty." And some, he noted with just the slightest hint of what was to come, even seemed "jubilant" when they could be dishonest. Although it was only the fourth major Castro speech I had covered, I had heard and seen enough to tense up and wait for his next words. The tens of thousands of Cubans who had heard many more speeches than I had were also expectant. They knew something or someone *Yanqui* was going to be called out.

"We have no intention of using this rostrum to humiliate anyone in particular, even less when they are persons who have been authorized to enter the country," Castro said, his voice resounding throughout Havana's Chaplin Theater, where a specially-invited audience of would-be Latin American revolutionaries was seated. Behind Castro on the platform was a photograph two, maybe three, stories high of Che Guevara, Castro's guerrilla buddy who had mysteriously dropped from sight. Guevara's disappearance had set off rumors that he and Castro had serious differences. But the giant Guevara photo and the fact that Castro had made Che's dictum that "The Duty of Every Revolutionary Is to Make Revolution" into a national slogan belied that idea. Besides, Guevara had been designated honorary chairman of the guerrilla conference he was not attending.

Fidel Castro addresses the General Assembly of the United Nations in New York in 1960.

Castro added: "Is it not perhaps being extremely naive to believe that the CIA is a perfect, wonderful, very intelligent organization incapable of making the slightest blunder?" Castro pointed a finger in the air for emphasis, a trademark indicating he was heading for one of his crescendos. But he was not there yet. First a little laughter. And he got it when he said sarcastically that he could not "criticize anybody wavering before such evident facts ... like the one who said he was not a judge." His audience now knew who the anybody was. So did I. But Cuba's leader felt I deserved a better label than just anybody. "Que magnifico muchacho (great guy/boy)," he said, drawing even more laughter from the gathering of delegates and special guests at Cuba's first and, as it has turned out, last formal pro-guerrilla conference. Even the few guests who spoke only English knew he was being sarcastic. Biologically, Castro was one year younger than I. Politically, he was years older.

"Really, the AP trains its little cadres well," he said, drawing more laughter. "But if some really want to see up to what point they are judges or not, let them analyze everything they write daily and they will see how impartial they are." He added, "We have been reading the news of that agency for eight years, which is always at the service of the imperialists, always hiding something, defending something which is never right not even by mistake distorting everything." So Castro disliked the AP before I got to Cuba. Why, then, did he let me in? Why did he continue receiving and reading AP news? Did he think it would be a measure of the climate in Washington?

For a minute I felt better. Maybe he would suffer me after all. Then Castro got to a favorite theme, the United States' many attempts to bring down Cuba's Revolution, this time by landing a CIA assassination team armed with special bullets to kill him. He said such bullets were banned "even in all-out war." Angrily, he declared, "We directly accuse the U.S. government and hold it responsible for these acts."

The crowd, as if on cue, interrupted him with shouts of "Fidel hit the Yankees hard." They were words I was to hear at many Castro speeches. "We accuse President (Lyndon) Johnson and hold him directly responsible." And he might as well have added that any American journalist currently based in Cuba who didn't believe Johnson and the U.S. government were to blame was either extremely naive or in cahoots with the CIA.

So, after six months, my presence in Cuba was no longer unnoticed nationally and obviously not very welcome. Comandante (Major) Fidel Castro Ruz, First Secretary of the Central Committee of the Communist Party of Cuba and Prime Minister of the Revolutionary Government, had given me an introduction that invariably preceded his speeches and put out an unfriendly assessment of me not only to Cubans but also to Latin America and to anywhere Radio Havana could be heard.

He had done something else I did not recognize then: He had seeded suspicion that I was perhaps a Pentagon spy or at the very least a plant for the Central Intelligence Agency. Obviously Castro had no proof, otherwise I would have been in the hands of the Department of State Security (DSE) instead of struggling through his two-hour speech. Although he had used the name CIA more than a dozen times in his speech before he got to me, his use of the word "cadre" should have been the tip off to me that in his thinking he was linking the two.

I was a little puzzled by his choice of the word "cadre" but dismissed it as a sign the Cuban Foreign Ministry had done a poor job in researching my background. Cadre was a word I normally associated with things military, and I hadn't given a salute to anybody since I was discharged from the U.S. Navy at the end of World War II. What I didn't perceive was just how widely the word had been adopted and used by communism, often to denote a core group of elite political specialists. These included informers, spies and double agents. That was true of the Soviet KGB, whose agents frequently went undercover as journalists. Take the case of the first KGB man in Havana. He reportedly operated publicly as a representative of Tass, the Soviet news agency. I knew a third secretary at the Soviet Embassy in Havana who later turned up in Lisbon during the Portuguese revolution as a Tass reporter.

I discovered much later that people working in and for Cuban intelligence and counter-intelligence also found the word "cadre" handy. And so did Guevara. He used the word in his diary, describing the organization and management of guerrilla groups in Bolivia.

Had I known all those things at the time Castro spoke on August 10, 1967, I would have been even more concerned about my future in Cuba. I had come to understand almost from the day I landed in Havana that, as the newest resident AP correspondent, I would be on trial as a potential enemy or spy. There was something else I was soon to discover about being the only American journalist based in Cuba. I was the only available U.S. target on the island. If Castro lashed out at the United States in a speech or if there was a question about U.S. actions in Vietnam, the cameras focused on me. Even anti-Castro Cubans often thought I had some connection with Washington.

Still, for the most part, I was simply dumbfounded by Castro's anger at me and the blatant official reaction it had ignited. The day after the speech, technicians came to the AP apartment "to adjust and repair" a telephone that I already suspected had been bugged.

Havana movie houses quickly began showing newsreels that included Castro's reference to me as the "magnifico muchacho." I felt I was being watched more closely than ever by members of the Committees for the Defense of the Revolution — the neighborhood watch groups. Then came an attack in the communist youth newspaper, *Juventud Rebelde* (Rebel Youth). A crude cartoon on the front page showed me on a toilet with feces coming out of my mouth. It looked like something out of *Mad* magazine. For a moment, I almost laughed. But, alongside the cartoon, the newspaper carried a headline informing readers of an accompanying analysis (something Castro had suggested in his speech) of my reporting, tiitled, "The Adventures and Exploits of a Magnificent Muchacho." A subhead warned I was "an unforgettable personality." Clumsy as it was, it was somewhat less worrisome than Castro's words. The newspaper often went to the extreme to interest and arouse its younger readers.

I quieted some of my fears by noting that the official Cuban Communist Party newspaper *Granma* had published the text of Castro's speech without added comment about me. I also found some comfort in rereading the part of his speech where he said that despite "lying truculent fraudulent news agencies ... courtesy compels us to treat

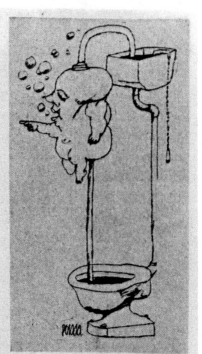

Un personaje inolvidable de OLAS

Las aventuras y proezas de un magnífico muchacho

En este mundo traidor
nada es verdad ni mentira
todo es según el color
del cristal con que se mira
SU LEMA PREFERIDO

El discurso de Fidel

Por FENTON WHEELER

LA HABANA, agosto 11 (AP).—Fidel Castro afirmó anoche que el presidente Johnson es responsable de una conspiración para asesinarlo, acusó a elementos del Partido Comunista venezolano de traición, y criticó a los países comunistas que han prestado ayuda financiera y técnica a gobiernos "oligárquicos" como los de Colombia.

Castro acusó anoche al Presidente de los Estados Unidos de ser responsable de un frustrado complot para darle muerte, dijo que la Agencia Central de Inteligencia

NOTA No. 1.—Obsérvese como el "magnífico" presenta en primer plano la posibilidad de un atentado, y deja entrever la preocupación personal de Fidel, por ese hecho.

NOTA No. 2.—En otro párrafo presenta nuevamente a los infiltrados capturados como

Cuban newspaper *Rebel Youth* front pages its reaction to Fidel Castro's sarcastic referral to John Fenton Wheeler in a speech as a "magnifico muchacho" (great guy) and who Castro added was trained by the Associated Press to distort news about Cuba.

persons with politeness, but courtesy does not compel us to keep from saying some truths which are widely known."

Castro had been displeased with the AP many times before I arrived in Havana. But I was singled out for a public rebuke because two days earlier I refused to declare that two Cuban exiles being presented under guard at a news conference were in fact CIA agents sent to kill Castro. The exiles allegedly had confessed earlier that they were working for the CIA and had been sent to Cuba with bullets tipped with potassium cyanide. During a nationally televised press conference at the pro-guerrilla, pro-revolution conference of the Organization of Latin American Solidarity (OLAS), which was held in the big room at the Havana Libre (ex-Hilton) hotel, Cuban President Osvaldo Dorticós said he was concerned that questions from some of the more than 20 visiting U.S. reporters covering the Havana meeting indicated they had doubts the captured Cubans were in fact agents of the CIA.

"How can any honest man have the slightest doubt?" Dorticós demanded. Then he said he wanted to "poll" the U.S. press on the matter. It probably was the first and last poll in Castro history. The first replies to Dorticós' question came from the leftist and anti-war press, including *Worker*, the *National Guardian*, the *Monthly Review*, the *Militant Rat* magazine, and the *Liberation News Service*. One by one, those reporters rose from their seats to say they believed the captured men were either CIA agents or CIA mercenaries.

Dorticós' real targets of the poll, however, were the two U.S. news agencies — AP and United Press International (UPI). Castro distrusted UPI for having reported in 1956 that he had been killed. Using erroneous information from a Batista general, UPI reported that Castro had been killed at the start of Castro's guerrilla campaign, an insurgency that eventually tumbled the Batista dictatorship and brought Castro to power. Castro thought the AP had slighted his struggle to overthrow Batista and had misreported and misjudged his rule since then. Both agencies often drew official scorn.

UPI's correspondent was a Cuban, Pedro Bonetti, an understandably cautious reporter from his point of view. He wanted to take his family and leave the country. Eventually Castro would let him. But on that day, knowing that Castro would be rating his reply, Bonetti could not afford to go against the political grain. He said he accepted the evidence as presented. I knew what was coming next. "What about the Associated Press?" Dorticós asked.

My Spanish was still limited at the time, but even if it had been perfect I would have made the same reply. "I am a journalist, not a judge," I said and sat down. The only sound I remember was a voice of approval over my shoulder, the unmistakable accent of Gordon Martin of the British Broadcasting Corporation saying "hear, hear." The rest of the 200 to 300 people in the room were silent.

Dorticós was not happy with my response. I had unintentionally failed to address him as "Mr. President," as some other journalists had. This was probably considered rude and insulting. But, journalistically, so was his poll. For the moment, however, he could do nothing about my answer. He questioned a few more American reporters and then, smiling, said he understood why some journalists were unwilling "to make judgments on the spot." Therefore, he said American reporters going back to the United States —

meaning everybody but me — should ask President Johnson "what he knows about this."

Castro clearly was not happy with my answer and said so during his speech at the closing the OLAS conference. That was the case even though I had filed a story the day Dorticós polled the press, saying that six men, including the two confessed would-be assassins, who earlier had been presented to foreign reporters, had admitted they were recruited and trained by the CIA and were on a mission to kill Castro.

In his speech, Castro had also quoted from a Miami-datelined AP story: "The band of infiltrators was described today in Miami by its leader Major Armando Fleites as on a mission to kill Prime Minister Fidel Castro, which would form part of a campaign of irregular warfare designed to overthrow the communist regime." And then Castro added, "Is it that the government of the United States doesn't feel responsible for these acts?"

At first I kidded myself with the idea that perhaps I was merely a convenient outlet for frustration Castro might have felt over the outcome of his pro-guerrilla meeting. Minor disagreement had cropped up among the 27 nations attending the Havana meeting before Castro got it smoothed over. That fuss centered on commercial dealings with non-communist Latin American countries by the Soviet Union Cuba's key financial supporter. Another dispute arose over the Venezuelan Communist Party's lack of support for a Castro-style guerrilla movement in its homeland. Both were an embarrassment of a sort for Castro and delayed the conference closing for a couple of days.

But, worse yet, they distracted attention from the conference theme — another Guevara slogan calling on revolutionaries around the world and especially in Latin America to create "two, three, many Vietnams" and thus defeat "U.S. aggression and imperialism." Guevara's call to arms had been made public in Havana nearly four months before the OLAS meeting. At my first news conference in Havana, I recall a smirking army officer Capt. Osmany Cienfuegos, head of an African-Asian solidarity organization called OSPAAL, announcing Guevara's message calling for many Vietnams. Cienfuegos presented Guevara's message as if it had just arrived. However, the message may have been written and left in Havana before he disappeared to try to start a Castro-style guerrilla war in Bolivia. The captain turned aside all questions about Guevara's whereabouts.

Preceding the OLAS conference, Castro, as he had done every year in the early days of the Revolution, declared 1967 "the Year of Heroic Vietnam." Guevara's face was emblazoned across Havana in preparation for the OLAS meeting. Special guests included U.S. black power advocate Stokely Carmichael and a tiny Viet Cong heroine who was reported to have killed more than a dozen American servicemen fighting in her homeland. There were special delegations of the North Vietnamese and the Viet Cong.

Carmichael had called for black guerrilla-style uprisings in the United States. Castro embraced him and publicly referred to him simply as "Stokely." President Dorticós joined in. Referring to news stories of racial violence in Detroit and New York that summer, he accused the United States of a "genocide against Negroes."

Delegates at the OLAS meeting were read a message from Douglas Bravo, the Venezuelan guerrilla leader, but Guevara did not make an appearance. Castro's guerrilla-model friend and adopted co-patriot was struggling to start a revolution in Bolivia, and the Bolivian army was closing in on him. Castro surely knew Guevara was in trouble, probably as he spoke to the guerrilla delegates in Havana.

Looking back after all these years, I wonder if what angered Castro most about my reply in the Dorticós poll was my failure to appreciate how many times and how many ways the CIA had tried to assassinate him or immobilize him — how at least three U.S. presidents had approved such attempts in the first eight years Castro was in power, and how the CIA was still trying to kill him. So what if the group of Cubans paraded before the OLAS conference were a ragtag bunch whose answers to questions from reporters were sometimes hesitant or seemed rehearsed? So what if they had unexplainably risked their operation by bringing American-labeled cans of fruit and soup along with their special bullets and fancy radio equipment? Castro knew there had been several CIA attempts to eliminate him, even if I didn't. Some of the most harebrained of these included making his beard fall out, doctoring his cigars with a chemical so he would hallucinate during a speech, and trying to poison his favorite milkshake.

The irony for me in assassination conjecturing was that, during the time I was to cover Cuba, the story I feared most was that somebody would try, maybe even succeed, in killing Castro, and I would have to try to get such news out of the country. I felt sure I would have been arrested, even though

I deplore assassination in any form. There may have been another factor: In communist countries, almost all journalists are agents of the government at some level. The 11 Soviet journalists based in Havana when I got there were either KGB agents outright or KGB informants. The same was true for the reporters of East Bloc nations. Journalists of Prensa Latina, the Cuban news agency, were also beholden to report to their government.

Castro had known of American journalists who later turned out to be working for the CIA. He may simply have seen my answer to Dorticós as just what a CIA agent masquerading as a journalist would reply. If Castro said the CIA was involved, it was prudent for those in Havana to believe him.

Then, suddenly, the official criticism of me died out. A Reuters colleague said he had heard that visiting foreign journalists had told Cuban officials there they thought the government was overdoing its attacks on me. One of the names mentioned was Lee Lockwood, who had just published a long interview with Castro in *Playboy* magazine and was said to have some access to Castro. I doubted Lockwood had intervened at any level. But whatever the government's motive, I was relieved the public criticism had stopped. I got an emotional lift when the Israeli ambassador came to my office in his official car to congratulate me on my answer to Dorticós and give me a carton of English cigarettes. I began thinking that Castro had measured me as no more than a political gnat, something to be brushed aside and forgotten. Was my brief notoriety over? Or was I as naive as Castro had suggested?

Chapter Two

GETTING TO HAVANA

$\mathbf{A}$t the age of seven, in the year 1932, I decided I was a Republican. My father was a Republican, along with, it seemed, almost everybody else in Kansas. I remember sitting on a Lincoln Grade School swing, arguing with my boyhood friend, Karl Horner, after the election of Franklin D. Roosevelt.

Karl was a Democrat. He was for Roosevelt. Karl's father was the janitor at the school. I was for Hoover. My father was the editor and owner of the *Abilene Chronicle*, a morning newspaper with a history for reporting local news in tough times. The *Chronicle* was the first newspaper in Abilene. It had covered the town's Wild West days, when it was a dusty cowboy capital at the end of the Chisholm Trail, sporting booze, gambling, prostitution, gunplay, and a marshal named Wild Bill Hickok.

The newspaper had a lot of history but not much else when my father bought it. It was going broke under the ownership and operation of J. G. Oliver. Everybody called him "Dad" Oliver, and he was said to be a "nice old guy." But Abilene's other newspaper, the *Reflector*, was beating him.

The *Reflector* came out in the evening and had some money behind it. Its editor-owner, Charlie Harger, was a well-known Republican who always attended the party's national conventions. He was also influential among a circle of small-town Kansas newspapermen who customarily patted each other on the back and saw to it that their readers got all the news they deemed fit to print. That news included stories from the Associated Press.

But the *Chronicle* couldn't afford AP news. It had to depend on local news. When my father took over, the newspaper boasted one linotype, a cylinder printing press, a couple of beat-up roll-top desks, two typewriters, and not much else. My father paid $9,960 for the newspaper on May 1, 1929. Four months later, the Great Depression struck. The mortgage on the *Chronicle* that Dad Oliver held at a pre-Depression 6 per cent interest rate cost my father $83 a month to keep the paper afloat. That amount of money was no small potatoes in those days, when potatoes often were among the produce used by farmers to pay for a *Chronicle* subscription. People were hard up, and I remember more than once asking my father why a certain store had suddenly closed. "Went broke" was always his answer.

My family survived better than most. We got a good portion of our groceries barter-style from the few stores that advertised in the *Chronicle*. Nobody in Abilene had any money to speak of, except the town's three bank presidents and C. L. Brown, the millionaire who had a utilities monopoly, a big park south of town, a comparatively modest house for a man of his wealth, and a white Pierce Arrow with those fancy headlights in the front fenders.

Karl, who wore blue overalls to school, said Hoover had caused the Depression, and that was why Roosevelt had won the presidency. I wore striped overalls like the railroad men. Those cost a little more, but my mother insisted I not appear in just plain blue denim. I said Hoover had not caused the Depression; something called stocks had. That, more or less, was our entire political disagreement. In latter years, Karl became more conservative, and I went the other way.

My father's journalistic experience consisted of being a job printing salesman. But along the way he had been a high school principal, so he knew English, and he liked Kansas history. My mother was "old Abilene," a native. Once she had gone to California on a brief trip as a schoolgirl. Few of her friends were that widely traveled. She had inherited her family's home, so we had a good place to live. It had been built by her father, Orlando Parks Fenton, an early Abilene feed dealer. The big white house occupied a good portion of the former property of one of the town's early land developers, Thomas C. Henry, who was, for a time, known as the "wheat king of Kansas."

But the house had a more interesting piece of history. It sat on a corner fronting Buckeye Street, once the Chisholm Trail. The other side of the house faced a street far more exciting to me or any boy who ever played cowboy. Before being renamed First Street, it had been the notorious Texas Street, where the cowboy saloons and the shooting used to be.

Had I been better versed in local history, I could have imagined Marshal Hickok walking down my street. My father surely must have, for he published a booklet in 1938 titled "Early Days in Abilene." He had done it with the cooperation of 93-year-old J. B. Edwards, a former *Chronicle* reporter who had arrived in Abilene as a young man in 1870, one year before Hickok showed up. Edwards had written this for the *Chronicle* about Wild Bill: "He had caused many men to die with their boots on, never taking any chances, but always either getting the drop on his man or shooting him down on any provocation. He stood over six feet high, straight as a man could be formed (we have never seen a better formed person), quick as a flash, the best shot with a pistol on the frontier. His hair long, hanging down to his shoulders, tasty in his dress, his complexion fair as any woman's, such was the chosen one to keep peace in our midst."

The description was subjective but probably accurate. Edwards also reported that Hickok had killed two men in Abilene, one a lawman he shot by mistake. I had heard from somebody that he did this standing at my corner, firing one gun down Texas Street and the other down Buckeye Street at the same time. Of course it wasn't true, but it made for good boyhood lore. So, once in a while, when we played cowboy games, somebody pretended to be Hickok. But mostly we concentrated on trying to act like the movie heroes of our times, Tom Mix or Buck Jones.

In my early boyhood some of the old wooden buildings on First Street retained their false fronts. A horse trough still held water near where the Alamo saloon, Abilene's fanciest tavern, had stood. The trough was fed by a city water spigot, and I took a drink from it every time I passed by. It was good water. At one time it had been bottled and sold as "Abilena Water," which was said to be 1/100th of a percent purer than Ivory soap, which claimed 99.98 percent purity. I could only wonder about that and where the Bull's Head Elkhorn Pearl and other saloons had been.

There was one thing I did know about a livery stable within smelling distance of my back door. It had big black mules and wagons that delivered groceries until the Depression forced the business to an end. Just a block from my house was the site of storied Drovers Cottage, where cattle barons and buyers sometimes shared space with Abilene's orneriest. The hostelry alongside the Kansas Pacific (later Union Pacific) railroad tracks best marked the end of the trail that long route cowboys took through Texas and Oklahoma to drive their cattle for sale in Abilene.

The town fathers enjoyed the money that the Texas drovers spent raising hell in Abilene. But after a couple of years they tired of the saloon-sinning and became more pious. In the early 1870s they suggested the cowboys quit celebrating in Abilene and move farther west with the railroad to Ellsworth or Dodge City. By the time I was growing up, my once desirable part of town was on the "wrong side" of the tracks.

So was Karl's and the home of another Abilene family named Eisenhower. In fact, the Eisenhower home, now a national archive, stands just across the Santa Fe railroad tracks that still abut Karl's old home. Those tracks were so close that I remember how Karl's house shook whenever a freight train went by. The Eisenhower home was a little farther away from the rail line but faced Lincoln school. The father of a future president of the United States sometimes had to chase boys from his yard when softballs from the school came too near to his front porch. I never hit one that far.

I had not heard much hometown talk about Dwight Eisenhower until after he announced to the world in November 1942 that an Allied invasion force had landed in North Africa. But my sister, being a girl and therefore more conversant with our mother, had. Years later she said that when she was a young girl she had seen a man in military uniform walking smartly by our house on the way to the center of town. When she asked my mother who he was, my mother dismissed him as not being important, saying "that's just Dwight Eisenhower. He's in the Army."

Then my mother added that when her older sister, my favorite aunt Daisy Belle, was young, she had gone on a double date that included Dwight Eisenhower. The two young men brought Daisy Belle home last and late from an ice cream social or some such. It was already nine p.m., about an hour later than promised, and Daisy's escort was too skittish to take her to the front door. Young Eisenhower sat in the buggy and waited. This infuriated my maternal grandmother, who was watching from the bay window. Under her social code, she held Eisenhower equally to blame for bad manners and barred Daisy Belle from future dates that included either of the young men. People did that back then. Had the cowboys still been around, they surely would have hooted.

After World War II, when Eisenhower became president and Abilene became famous but not notorious again, the city fathers built what they called "Old Abilene Town" next to the abandoned Rock Island depot. It could not of course come close to the real thing. Nonetheless, the recreated town became a tourist draw, riding on the coattails of the Eisenhower Center and Memorial and the Eisenhower Presidential Library. The old Eisenhower house is at its same site. But Lincoln school and its red bricks are long gone. So is the old red stone Dickinson County courthouse, with its oiled wooden floors and brass spittoons, its giant elm trees, and its green wooden benches, all of which used to be across from my front door. The new courthouse looks like a small town medical clinic.

By the time I was 11 I suppose I still was a nominal Republican. My first train trip, for example, came when my father took the family to Topeka to hear Alfred M. Landon accept the Republican nomination to oppose Roosevelt in 1936. My dad said Landon sometimes had dropped by the *Chronicle* office, and the two of them would sit on newsprint rolls in the basement of the newspaper and discuss things, probably FDR and politics. My father was very excited by Landon's nomination, although I suspect he didn't think Landon had much of a chance to win. He was stunned, however, when the Kansas governor couldn't even carry his own state and Roosevelt won what was to be his biggest victory in four presidential elections.

That summer I began sweeping out the *Chronicle* office early in the morning. That task turned me away from journalism somewhat because it also meant sweeping the sidewalk in front of the newspaper, where hundreds of bugs had been attracted the night before by the neon marquee at the Plaza movie house next door. In the spring of 1940 I began working part-time as a printer's devil. Republicans be damned, the Roosevelt administration had improved the national economy and things in Abilene, too.

Besides its prime job of reporting the local news, the *Chronicle* now ran a steady printing business to help keep it alive It also was gaining in circulation on the other newspaper. I was just learning how to locate type letters in the tray and put them in a job stick when France capitulated to Hitler. Nick Carter, the shop foreman, heard about it on the radio while feeding paper into the old gas-powered Kelly job press. He stopped the hissing press, looked across at me, and said he hoped the United States would not get into a war.

A few nights that summer I carried proofs at the *Chronicle*. Sometimes I read them, but I had little interest in the editorial function of the newspaper. I enjoyed helping Al Makins, however. He was a college man who had become my father's chief reporter, writer, copy editor, and often proof reader. He had another task, one in which I could help — running about a block at nine-thirty at night to throw a bag of *Chronicles* destined for country subscribers on the train.

By the time I was a senior in high school, World War II was nearly a year old. Al Makins was in the Army getting gold bars and being trained to die on Omaha Beach. I no longer had any political affiliation, except being an American. I joined the Navy for three years. While I was there, my father merged the *Chronicle* with the *Reflector*. He widened his interests in state politics, becoming a press advisor to Governor Andrew Schoeppel, a Kansas Republican. My father's name, C. W. "Red" Wheeler, became better known across the state when he began spending more time in the state capital as chairman of the State Board of Education. I think he was getting ready to go into state politics.

I received an honorable discharge from the Navy, though virtually unmedaled. Nineteen days later my father had a heart attack and died in my arms. We lost the newspaper under an ironclad agreement that allowed the *Reflector* owner Harger to buy us out for peanuts. My father, 30 years Harger's junior, had bet he would outlive him. I left the *Chronicle* having reported only one story, a Memorial Day piece about the few additional graves that Abilene servicemen occupied in the cemetery. Many of those killed had been buried where they died, land or sea.

My father had counted on me going to journalism school, so I did. I first went to the University of Missouri, where I couldn't handle French and then to the University of Kansas, where I switched to Spanish.

My first job was on the *Topeka Capital*, the newspaper of ultra-conservative Republican Sen. Arthur Capper. He liked to pat 4-H girls and drooled his milk down his vest. I stayed at the *Capital* for about two years, marveling at the way management politicized the news. By then I was far out of step in Topeka, having become a Democrat and having cast my first presidential vote for Harry Truman. My second presidential vote was for Adlai Stevenson, against Abilene's favorite son, Dwight D. Eisenhower. My third vote was the same, when both men opposed each other again in 1956.

By the time Castro came to power at the start of 1959, I had been working on newspapers ten years and was the news editor of the evening paper in Corpus Christi, Texas. I remember that a couple of Associated Press executives came to Corpus Christi to explain to my bosses why the AP had been slow and sloppy (my adjectives) in reporting the fall of the Batista dictatorship in Cuba and Castro's takeover. The news service executives, I was told, were on a tour explaining to several client newspapers why the AP had fumbled the story. Clearly, it had been a case of bad reporting from Havana.

The case sparked my interest in foreign reporting. That interest grew in 1961, when Castro's army overwhelmingly defeated the forces of the CIA-staged invasion at the Bay of Pigs. I was shocked that President John F. Kennedy had embarked the United States on such a militaristic venture, even taking into account Washington's Cold War fever and the U.S. anger over Castro communism. The 1962 Cuban missile crisis both alarmed and frightened me. Then the U.S. escalation in Vietnam sprouted, and I started to think seriously about trying to get a foreign reporting job, preferably in a Spanish-speaking country.

After thirteen years on newspapers, I managed a one-year journalism scholarship at the University of Chile in Santiago. I was there in November 1963, when John F. Kennedy was assassinated. I noted that several stories linked assassin Lee Harvey Oswald with Cuba. I doubted their veracity. I didn't think Castro would risk such a venture.

Five months later, when I went to work for the Associated Press in Columbus, Ohio, I began learning about life in a wire service. I told my bosses I wanted to go into foreign service. So, after a year, I was transferred to the AP foreign desk in New York City, where foreign editor Nate Polowetsky liked to claim 12 months in his domain equaled an entire college education. That experience certainly outclassed journalism school.

After some months in Polowetsky's academy, the AP's general manager and president Wes Gallagher called me into his office and told me I was going to Cuba. He asked if I had any Cuban connections. I remembered my father smoked Roi-Tans when he could afford them, and they must have contained a little Cuban tobacco back then. But I said no I had no Cuban connections of any kind, meaning, in my view, that I was neither for nor against Castro. Gallagher said good luck, goodbye, and that I had 10 days to get to Havana.

Chapter Three

DATELINE HAVANA

A Britannia turbojet of Cubana de Aviacion landed us at Havana's Jose Marti International airport after a flight from Mexico City on February 13, 1967. Five days earlier, the U.S. State Department had validated my passport for "one round trip to Cuba." I didn't need U. S. approval to get into Cuba, but I might need that stamp in my passport if I wanted to re-enter the United States without problems.

Travel to Cuba by U.S. citizens had been prohibited by the State Department after President Eisenhower broke diplomatic relations with Castro's government early in 1961. The United States took that step after the revolutionary leader nationalized all foreign companies in Cuba. U.S. journalists were exempted from the State Department travel ban and could go to Cuba if Castro would let them in.

My wife at that time had the same State Department stamp in her passport and the same edgy feeling as we passed through Cuban immigration and customs. It had started at the Cuban consulate in Mexico City, where we felt certain the CIA had photographed us as we left with Cuban tourist visas. Cuban security in Havana may have done the same thing as we walked toward immigration and customs, stepping first into boxes of white powder so our shoes, we were informed, could not bring hoof and mouth disease into Cuba. Everybody official was quiet but not unfriendly as we claimed our luggage. Some of them undoubtedly also knew that suddenly we had become the only Americans who would be "legally" residing in Cuba. None of the other departing passengers talked to us.

Ann herself was another novelty. Wives of AP correspondents, as a rule, did not accompany their husbands to Cuba after Castro took power. The rest of the Western press corps and nearly all of the East Bloc journalists were either single or had left their spouses behind.

The ride from the airport on Ranco Boyeros Avenue mirrored what eight years of Castro's revolution had done to the Cuban capital. Nearly everything along the way — the road itself, street lights, signs, buildings and taxis — needed repair. That included the faded clothing that many people wore. One exception were those Cubans in uniform. But almost everything American-made needed fixing. The few automobiles were mostly spacious 1950s models with wide comfortable seats and tail fins, and the fact that they were still running was a tribute to Cuban mechanical ingenuity.

Along with the end of U.S.-Cuban diplomatic relations had come a U.S. economic boycott against Cuba. It had stopped all American products from entering Cuba. Castro called it a blockade, not a boycott. He would denounce it for many years to come. The United Nations also has condemned it. But back in the late 1960s, it was just beginning to take its toll on people's lives. Few people walked around with smiles on their faces. Nevertheless, downtown Havana had kept its charm, seedy as it was.

The apartment used by the AP also had some charm. Big, light, and airy, its eighth-floor terrace overlooked the twin towers of the stately old Hotel Nacional and the Malecon the seashore drive that ran along the Havana waterfront. If you craned your neck to the left, you could see the base of what once supported a statue honoring the American battleship the U.S.S. Maine. With the cry "Remember the Maine," the United States had declared war on Spain in 1898 after a mysterious explosion blew up the Maine in Havana's harbor. The war freed Cuba from Spain but put the island under U.S. domination for 60 years.

On January 18, 1961, about two weeks after Eisenhower broke diplomatic relations with Cuba, the Council of Ministers, whose presiding officer was Castro, ordered the eagle atop the statue removed as "a symbol of U.S. imperialism." It was one in a series of acts protesting U.S. intervention in Cuba. Looking slightly to the right from the terrace, one could see the entrance to Havana harbor. In the background El Morro Castle was visible. Near it was La Cabana, the infamous prison fort where Fulgencio Batista, the dictator who the United States had allowed to function before Castro ousted him, sometimes held his political prisoners. Batista reportedly threw some of those young, Castro-aged dissidents to the sharks. Once in power, Castro, too, had imprisoned dissidents he labeled as "counter-revolutionaries" in La Cabana.

If I stood on the terrace at the AP apartment early in the morning, I could look down a floor to the right and sometimes see Rene Portocarrero, one of the Castro Revolution's adopted painters, enjoying the sunrise and a smoke on his terrace. We usually nodded but seldom spoke. One bedroom of the AP apartment was filled with broken furniture and dead American television sets. Only half of the bathrooms and even less of the electric stove in the kitchen worked. The refrigerator was held together with hurricane tape. There was water only one hour a day, none of it drinkable. There was no air conditioning, but usually there was a sea breeze.

None of the furniture in the living room had legs. But the room boasted two genuine, though aging, tiger-skin rugs, complete with heads leftover from a previous AP correspondent who had been in India. The wall paint was peeling and what curtains there were hung in shreds. There were no toilet seats in the bathrooms. As time passed, I would discover that many public places had no toilet seats. I asked people why on several occasions, but nobody seemed to know. Everyone in a capital that in pre-Castro days was known as "the Pearl of the Antilles" must have been sitting on porcelain.

Along with a 60-gallon oil drum used to store water, we inherited an apartment maid. Ramona was a fountain of common sense, hard work and good will. Undoubtedly, she had to report to the government about activities and visitors to the AP apartment, but I felt certain then and now that her reports were fair and without malice. She and Ann became good friends almost immediately.

The apartment had one professional advantage. Provided the elevator was working, it was only a minute away from the Associated Press office around the corner. At No. 4 Calle 21, the ground-floor office was just down the street from the Hotel Capri, where remaining slivers of the lobby curtains did nothing to block the heat of the Havana sun, and the air conditioning was another casualty of Castro's hated U.S. economic blockade. In Batista's days, I was told, the lobby was icy cool, one of the capital's deluxe hangouts for U.S. crime bosses, gamblers, pimps and New York-Miami-type tourists.

Like the AP apartment, the office was roomy. It boasted a teletype room with equipment to receive radio signals that brought the AP news wire translated into Spanish to Cuba. It was passed on to Cuban customers, including Castro. The radio equipment could only receive news, not transmit it. There was also a darkroom alongside outdated wire-photo transmission-receiving equipment, and a locked and abandoned *New York Times* office, empty except for old (invaluable to me) copies of *Bohemia*, the Cuban national news magazine. The office of the correspondent was endowed with a private bathroom, which had running water most of the time.

Our lifeline to the AP — a creaking Western Union pre-Castro machine — was connected to the downtown Havana Western Union office. From there my cables, as they were called then, would go to the AP cables (foreign news) desk in New York for editing and distribution around the world. There were mechanical problems, not surprisingly, with that tired, old communications system.

Western Union in Havana, like many government offices, also was frequently short of help. Western Union employees sometimes volunteered or were mandatorily "detached" to work in agriculture, especially during the cutting of sugar cane, Cuba's main income source.

Western Union service was very slow. Every Western correspondent's story also had to pass inspection by a government "reader" before it could be transmitted to its destination. Readers were not supposed to censor or change the wording, but they could and often did hold stories. After several unexplained delays, I confronted the Western Union manager one day at his office. I remember he suggested we go outside for a smoke. Out of earshot he said: "Wheeler, don't believe anything we tell you. If you call up and ask when your cables have left, we will give you a time they supposedly were sent, but it means nothing." I thanked him for his frankness and began the practice of sending each story in even shorter takes or sections, leaving anything I thought might be seen as sensitive to the very end of the story. Even so, I got delays of up to 48 hours before AP editors messaged me on the incoming AP news wire that they finally had received the story.

Someone from the Cuban Foreign Affairs Ministry had to come to the AP office to OK the caption on all AP photographs before we could transmit them by wire to AP New York. Delays were frequent. The AP news, including some internal messages, was distributed to nine subscribers in Havana, including the Palacio de la Revolucion, Castro's headquarters. So the government knew what the story looked like when it left and how it read when it came back translated into Spanish. I envied the few visiting journalists who came to Cuba during my time there. They could wait until they left Cuba to write pieces that might be critical and still put them under a Havana dateline. I couldn't.

Then there was the telephone. Because U.S. telephone giants would not accept the Cuban peso, theoretically equal with the dollar, according to Havana, I could only receive calls that had been prepaid in the United States. I couldn't call out. AP in New York called me if I alerted them by Western Union message ahead of time or if they thought there was a breaking story I needed to know about. Their calls were usually slow in coming in.

In 1967 the Vietnam war was the biggest story in newspapers and on prime-time television programs in the United States and much of the world, and the AP already had another "John Wheeler" writing from Vietnam. So, before I went to Havana, I had to find another name. So I used my middle name, "Fenton," which also was my mother's maiden name. When anyone addressed me as Fentone the Spanish pronunciation it indicated they knew the byline better than they knew me. The fact that they knew the byline at all was a pleasant surprise. AP reporters in foreign trenches often complained that many newspaper editors knocked their bylines off AP stories, either because it was the newspaper's policy, an editor's whim, or possibly to save one line of space. Wags said the agency's initials should have meant written by an "Anonymous Person," not by Associated Press. Castro knew better.

The Havana AP office, during my time, had six to 10 Cuban employees working seven days a week to distribute news and photos to Cuban government clients. None performed news functions. All were men, and two-thirds of them were black, which had made no difference to anybody in Cuba since Castro had taken over. Before Castro, there had been considerable racial discrimination coupled with but not tempered by widespread mixing, as evidenced by the multitude of mulattos across the island. Batista, for example, was a mulatto. The true social dividing line, however, always had been economic, separating the Spanish (the then U.S.-beholden rulers) and the economically elite from the thousands of poor, especially the *guajiros* (peasants) in the countryside. Castro had only one black man in his cabinet in 1967, Juan Almeida. But that was because Castro had restricted those posts almost exclusively to men who had fought with him or served in other areas as a revolutionary. And Almeida was among the best of those on both counts.

Every now and then one or two of the men in the Havana AP office would be asked to do volunteer work in agriculture. If they were on the government-approved list to leave Cuba for either the United States or Spain, heeding the volunteer call was virtually mandatory. Four eventually left Cuba. I recall portly Vicente Ochoa, one of the cheeriest men I ever met, coming back from sugar harvest soberer and 50 pounds lighter.

Another who eventually went to Spain was Esmond Grant Allen, a handsome white-haired man midway in his 60s and too old for cane-cutting. I inherited him and his 1952 Cadillac from the AP. Grant went with the office and was, of all things in communist Cuba, a hired chauffeur.

Both he and his car were relics from a time when he had made his living driving tourists to Havana's hotels and some of the capital's more sinful attractions. He was firmly anti-Castro and said so when he felt sure no one could hear him. He felt most useful when he drove Ann and me to diplomatic or official receptions. When there were places he thought it was too dangerous for him as a Cuban to go, I went alone in the Volkswagen Beetle that had been left in AP's care by the last New York Times correspondent to have been based in Havana.

The mainstay of the office was Stanley (Estanislaus) Graham. He tended the teletype machines and their clients, laboriously punched most of the AP cables going to Havana Western Union, and, once in a while, dictated my copy to New York. Though my stories sometimes caused him to wince, he never faltered. I was certain he was pro-Castro, but he never said so. If he was a Castro follower, he was also like many Cubans, anti-Washington certainly, but not anti-American. Castro's revolution had caused him hardships, but it had also allowed him and thousands of other blacks dignity and purpose. He was the hardest working and the best friend I had in the office. If Stanley had to "report" on me, I felt sure he would be accurate and, I hoped, fair. If others in the office staff were government informers, I could do little about it except hope they did not invent tales to please superiors.

If anyone in my office was spying, it certainly wasn't me. Later I learned the same did not apply to the Cuban Foreign Affairs Ministry and its foreign press section. On one of the first free weekends I had after arriving in Havana, Oscar

Lujones Gonzalez of the foreign press section invited me to go spear fishing. He was a good English speaker who said he had taken his honeymoon in the United States in pre-Castro days. He had obviously been assigned to befriend me and test my politics. Both of us knew it.

On a Sunday, Ann and I met him near the Havana Yacht Club that the government had taken over. Oscar had a boat available. It was at least a 40-footer. I asked if it had belonged to a club member who had gone to the United States. Oscar just smiled, shrugged, and helped Ann aboard. At sea, presumably within Cuba's declared 12-mile limit he gave me a quick briefing on spear fishing, then he and I jumped in. We were in only about fifteen feet of water. Oscar was shaped like a cube, but under water he was as graceful as the fish he hunted.

I pointed to a school of beautiful fish, each about three-feet long, and signaled to him that I was going to try my luck. He grabbed my arm and motioned for me to surface. Above water he told me the fish were barracudas and if I hit one the rest of the school probably would come after me. Back in the boat, Oscar gave me a bottle of rum and told me to wash the sea water out of my mouth. I think Oscar genuinely liked me, but I suspect he had a bigger motive in keeping me out of serious trouble that day. He did not want to be responsible for losing the only *Yanqui* correspondent in Cuba in the first weeks I was on the job. Maybe later such an incident might have been acceptable but not then.

On April 13, exactly two months after my arrival, I wrote to Ramiro del Río, the director of the foreign press section, asking to meet him and thanking Oscar Lujones for "his good acts." Shortly after that, Ann and I made a nine-day trip across the island eastward from Havana in the Volkswagen Beetle. Nobody bothered or questioned me, but I steered clear of anything that looked military except the Moncada barracks in the city of Santiago, where the blood-stained uniforms of Castro's defeated first rebel army were on display. I wrote a story about the trip and the people with whom I talked, briefly mentioning, among other things, the poor state of the Central Highway.

At a reception soon after the trip I met Del Rio. He wasted no time in telling me bluntly he disliked that story, particularly the part about potholes in the highway. He said he was just giving me some friendly advice. Hearing his words, I realized that the welcoming climate had changed for me. My time for "the treatment" was finished. I was moving toward the semi-enemy category.

The treatment (I learned that was what it was called only after I had left Cuba) involved ruses and deception employed by the government to mislead or misinform foreign journalists. If a journalist displayed pro-Castro sentiments, official help and sometimes favors were offered. The favors included special interviews, special trips across the island, or sex. If the journalist was deemed to be on the other side, a stone wall on news went up. Del Rio's attitude implied that there would be no more spear fishing trips for me. It seemed likely I had been classified as non-cooperative. Because I believed I had fallen into disfavor with the Cuban authorities, I tried to make sure the AP in Havana never did anything illegal.

On my first day at work, Grant began pestering me to have someone from Mexico bring parts for his 15-year-old Cadillac. One of the first stories I did was on how Cuba was struggling to trade around the U.S. economic blockade. In the mid-1960s the biggest Western trading partner of communist Cuba was General Francisco Franco's militantly anti-communist Spain. Madrid out-traded such Cuban communist brethren as East Germany, Bulgaria, Hungary, Romania, Poland, Yugoslavia, North Korea, and sometimes Czechoslovakia. Spanish trade approached that of Cuba's No. 2 trader, communist China. The Soviet Union, as everyone knew, was Cuba's biggest trading partner. The chief Western traders in those days of the Cold War were France, Canada, Britain, Japan, and Italy. Mexico was the only major Latin American trader.

With the blockade, there was no direct mail between Cuba and the United States. This revived an old journalistic device from the steamship days — the mailed story or "mailer." Every Thursday, a chartered plane carrying diplomatic correspondence from Western embassies in Havana flew to Nassau in the Bahamas. A courier from one of those embassies accompanied the correspondence and took it on to New York, where the diplomatic pouches were distributed to various embassy representatives there.

The Canadian embassy in Havana let me put my mailed stories in its diplomatic bag. AP picked them up in New York. I sent dozens, happy to avoid the prying eyes and delays of Western Union in Havana and able to write in something beside cablese, the old-time practice of running words together to decrease the word count on which telegraphic charges were based. After more than a year, the Canadians told me I was being observed by Cuban security each Wednesday when I delivered the mailers to their embassy. They said this was an embarrassment and they could no longer accept the stories. I went down the street to the Israeli embassy, which was under even tighter surveillance. They took the mailers without question. The Israelis were on Castro's unfriendly list in those days, despite having diplomatic relations with Havana. Castro finally ended relations with Israel in the 1970s.

Breaking news stories and Castro speeches had to be sent as spot copy. It was always a guess as to what time of day or night to ask the New York foreign desk to telephone me for a story on a Castro speech. Castro usually talked from two to four hours. I settled on asking for a call from New York 90 minutes after he began speaking, hoping by that time something newsworthy had developed.

Radio Havana broadcast Castro's speeches, and they were monitored and "storified" by the AP bureau in Miami, the center of anti-Castro exiles. I often disagreed with what Miami AP thought was important, and I particularly resented the New York AP foreign desk practice of including Miami paragraphs in my copy to get everything under a Havana dateline. I could see how AP editors in New York handled my stories when they were translated into Spanish but not in English, the version that was used in most of the rest of the world. Whenever I could, I included Castro's direct quotes in both Spanish and English to try to avoid something being skewed in translation. But, obviously, that couldn't be done for everything Castro said in those long, sometimes rambling speeches.

The news about Cuba that came out of Miami sometimes seemed to underscore Castro's contention that the AP was against him and a fountain of deliberately planted misinformation. To me, the Miami AP copy was certainly a pain in the neck, and although Castro had derided it publicly more than once, it never brought an official complaint from the Cuban government. Sending news that agreed with the government's version of happenings in Cuba had been no defense in the past however.

In his book *Bay of Pigs,* author Peter Wyden noted that UPI correspondent Henry Raymont's first accounts from Havana of the U.S-sponsored attack on the Cuban shore cast doubt on reports from UPI in Miami that the Castro regime was falling apart. Nonetheless, Raymont was arrested. I didn't know about that case as I started sending copy from Havana in 1967. But in my office Stanley Graham watched the incoming AP wire closely and was a reliable bellwether of possible trouble. After all these years, I can still picture him, a troubled look on his face, coming into my office with a Miami-datelined story and saying "Senor, just look at this."

During my stay in Cuba, however, there were no stories big enough to get me arrested. With the possible exception of the Mariel boat lift, there have been few top stories about Cuba since the U.S. defeat in 1961 at the Bay of Pigs and the 1962 missile crisis. And the reporting of those stories as they unfolded was almost exclusively from Washington, or, at times, from Moscow, but not Havana.

But there was one important story from Havana while I was there — a story that came to the front in 1968 and has lasted for almost four decades: Cuba's economic struggle and how its people suffered and survived.

Batista in 1952

Chapter Four

LEARNING ABOUT CASTRO

There were a lot of things I didn't know about Fidel Castro before I began working in Cuba. Among them was an appreciation of Castro's deep mistrust and, at times, outright hatred of the U.S. government and his constant suspicions about anything or anybody *Yanqui*. Nor did I appreciate his outrage at the repeated attempts by the U.S. Central Intelligence Agency to eliminate him either by assassination or overthrow. Had I known more about his student and guerrilla past, I would also have understood how he developed his fear of assassination, even before the CIA was created.

Castro's past spoke volumes filled with insights into his political motives and goals. People have written volumes about his ideas, his personality and his politics. When I arrived in Cuba, I certainly didn't know enough about any of these. Apparently the CIA never has, or if it has, its Cuba experts have either chosen to misread their information or ignore it. Otherwise, there would have been no Bay of Pigs adventure, no goofy or continuing attempts to eliminate Castro.

In his journey to power, Castro had learned to conspire, learned to disguise his true intentions when necessary, and learned to elude multiple attempts to kill him. Paranoia became a survival necessity for Castro after he began his political activism in the late 1940s and early 1950s and during his time as a guerrilla. He taught it to his followers. Friends and some enemies have agreed he also was blessed with a sixth sense for approaching danger.

Before he was twenty-one, Castro had developed a fear of betrayal, ambush and assassination. Long before the Central Intelligence Agency came into his life — as a student at Havana University, as a young lawyer-politician, and finally as an underground revolutionary — Castro quickly learned to respect and act on his fears. Havana University was a hotbed of politics violence and gangsterism. Rival factions could often be as dangerous for a blossoming dissident like Castro as the government police and the army. Student leaders were routinely tortured by police and sometimes killed. Castro armed himself as he rose to the forefront of university politics. There are many stories of how he dodged attacks from both political police and political rivals.

Two years after entering Havana University, Castro joined the Ortodoxo Party, the only party he belonged to before he founded his own movement. Castro had joined the Ortodoxos because he supported its founder, Sen. Eduardo "Eddy" Chibas, a leading vocal opponent of another corrupt and inept Cuban president, Ramon San Martin Grau. Castro followed Chibas for his politics and his radio attacks on the regime. The key element in his joining the party, according to Tad Szulc's book *Fidel: A Critical Portrait*, was because the party adopted the principles of the poet and Cuban independence icon Jose Marti.

Marti, to whom Castro has given credit as the great great grandfather of the Cuban Revolution, was killed in ambush in 1895 while trying to win Cuba's independence from Spain. Three years after Marti's death, Cuba did gain independence from Spain. But it was the United States' entry into the conflict after the battleship U.S.S. Maine was mysteriously blown up in Havana harbor that was decisive in finishing the guerrilla war Marti had started.

Castro revered Marti, with whom he identified as a rebel, as another son of a Spanish father and as a native of Oriente Province, where Castro chose to begin his armed revolt. But most of all, he admired Marti for his ideology, his fear of U.S. imperialism in Latin America, and his conclusion that only armed revolution would free Cubans from foreign control. When Castro went on trial for leading an assault on a Cuban army fort in 1953, six years before he came to power, he was asked by a military court who had planned the failed attack. He proudly told the court "the only intellectual author of this revolution is Jose Marti, the apostle of our independence."

Like Marti, Castro planned and organized his revolt from inside Cuba and from abroad. But he had no intention of being ambushed like Marti. Time and again he escaped from attempts to kill him.

Castro still remains a target of some of his ex-countrymen who reside in the United States and agitate for his demise, although their efforts are much less than those of nearly four decades ago. I have no idea what the CIA still is up to regarding Castro, but then I never did. Castro appears to have reined in some of his anti-Americanism since the death of the Soviet Union, maybe because it is economically expedient to do so, or perhaps he has mellowed with age to a less militant stance. But his hatred and distrust of Washington were at full strength when I was in Cuba. His feelings were heightened by the American involvement in Vietnam but based deeply on his experiences with the U.S. government. Then, too, there was the history of U.S.-Cuba relations long before he installed the Cuban Revolution.

After its defeat in the Spanish-American War, Madrid ceded control of Cuba to the United States. Technically, Cuba became a republic, but in reality it was a protectorate, often more like a colony. U.S. Marines were kept in Cuba until 1923. The U.S. exerted indirect control over the island under the Platt Amendment until President Franklin D. Roosevelt revoked it in 1934 as part of Washington's Good Neighbor Policy for Latin America. In fact, the United States still dominated Cuban politics.

U.S. policy on Cuba for the most part seemed linked to U.S. business. Washington usually paid little attention to politics in Havana unless American economic interests were affected. In those years Washington had not yet discovered human rights anywhere in Latin America. Cuba suffered through several dictatorships, all of them accepted by the United States government, especially if their authoritarian or often corrupt rulers were anti-communist. Meanwhile, the tourists poured into Havana from the States to enjoy the beaches, the rum, the sailing, the fishing, the gambling, the prostitution and the blue movies. The dollar was king. So were sugar and cigars, if you produced or sold them.

Fidel Castro was seven years old when Fugencio Batista, an army sergeant staged a military coup and became the power behind Havana's political throne for seven years. Batista oversaw Cuba's corrupt and ineffectual presidents while amassing a fortune, finally running for the office himself in 1940 and winning a four-year term. Then he retired to Florida at the end of his term in 1944.

A year later Castro entered law school at Havana University and into political thought. Hundreds of books have been written about Cuba and Castro since he came to power. There is wide disagreement over when he became a Marxist. In law school Castro emerged with leftist and a few populist sentiments. But people who knew him then and most book assessments, including those from anti-Castroites, agree he was not a member of communist organizations or the party at the university. As a Marti advocate at that time, Castro certainly would have been to the left of how Moscow viewed revolution in Latin America and definitely to the left of Cuba's staid and conventional pro-Soviet communists who had supported Batista in 1940 when he won the presidency.

In 1950 Batista returned to Cuba and formed a political party to try to return him to the presidency. Castro was married with a young son, still practicing politics and some law. His few clients were poor people who Castro felt had been abused by the ruling regime. Castro himself was not poor but was frequently on the edge of poverty because of his constant involvement in opposition politics.

On March 10, 1952 Batista tired of waiting for elections and seized power with help from his army buddies in a bloodless military coup. The takeover deposed President Carlos Prio Socarras and ended Fidel Castro's flirtation with conventional politics. Castro had been a candidate for congress when Batista grabbed power. Those elections, of course, were never held. Batista's coup, however, had more important consequences for Castro: They resolved any doubts he had about the need for armed revolution. He was now sure armed revolt was the only way to end the system of corrupt musical chairs and bring true independence to Cuba.

Castro began plotting to build what he envisioned as a rebel army. He went underground, staying a step ahead of Batista's political police and the army. He was seldom home, sleeping in the houses or apartments of friends, moving about Havana in different cars, soliciting money, trying to secure arms, and carefully screening and instructing recruits. His younger brother, Raul, a communist adherent some time before Castro became a Marxist, was among his inner circle.

Castro picked his first target far from Havana: the Moncada army barracks in Santiago, the country's second largest military installation. The idea was to take the barracks by surprise, seize its weapons, and then move into the Sierra Maestra (mountains) and begin a guerrilla war. If that attack failed, the mountains also would be a fall-back position in the province where Castro was born and his parents still lived on a big sugar farm. He could try again.

On July 26, 1953, Castro and his force of 120 rebels attacked the Moncada barracks, counting heavily on surprising the regiment. They were outnumbered four to one and out-gunned. A series of miscues ruined the element of surprise. Castro, his brother, and other rebels were captured, some tortured and executed brutally by Batista's soldiers. Others escaped and went into hiding. Castro was tried and convicted by a military court and sentenced to 15 years in prison, but he caught the nation's attention with his speech "History Will Absolve Me." He told the court he was guilty of nothing because the Moncada assault was a patriotic attack against a dictatorship that had seized power illegally.

Castro and two dozen of his rebels were sent to the prison in the Isle of Pines off Cuba's south coast. It was renamed the Isle of Youth after Castro won power and the prison left vacant and abandoned.

Castro again began organizing his rebel army, this time from inside the Isle of Pines prison. He continued his denouncement of the Batista regime. The pressure of an amnesty movement promoted by housewives, mothers and young people persuaded Batista to free Castro and his group in the spring of 1955. Within a month Castro had regrouped his inner circle of rebels into the organization that would finance and support Castro's guerrilla war. It was called the 26th of July Movement, named for the Moncada barracks attack. Castro has commemorated the date with a speech almost every year since he became Cuba's leader in 1959.

Four years before that, however, Castro decided he could not prepare a guerrilla army inside of Cuba. Also, he had stepped up his public attacks on Batista since his release from prison and now feared daily for his life. He began sleeping again in a different place every night, a practice he still followed at times during my days in Havana. Sometimes I was told, though never officially, that the practice was as much for recreation and rest as it was for security.

In the summer of 1955, Castro flew to Mexico to form and train a clandestine expeditionary force. Other rebels joined him. One non-Cuban who did was Ernesto "Che" Guevara, a young Argentine doctor who sought out Castro. Guevara was a theoretical Marxist at the time, but his revolutionary spirit had hardened after witnessing the CIA's ouster of the leftist government in Guatemala in 1954. The Guatemala event remains one of the few known CIA "successes."

Castro, through the 26th of July Movement that was operating in Cuba, had promised Cubans he would return in 1956 to fight for independence. On December 2, 1956, Castro and 80 men, including brother Raul and doctor Guevara, landed on the south coast of Cuba after a harrowing seven-day trip from Mexico aboard a reconditioned yacht designed to carry 25 persons. The yacht, "*Granma*," ran aground, missing its target and forcing Castro and his band to wade ashore. Guevara later called the arrival a shipwreck, not a landing. It was the first of several mishaps and escapes for Castro and his small guerrilla army.

Three days after landing, the exhausted party was resting and was nearly wiped out in an ambush by Batista's Rural Guards. But Castro and about 20 of his men survived.

After that narrow escape, Castro instructed his forces never to sleep in or near a structure where they could be ambushed, and he began to sleep with his rifle at his side, ready to fire.

As their beards grew, the guerrillas launched their war under the protection of the Sierra Maestra, aided at times with supplies from the 26th of July Movement, continual support from peasants, and a propaganda campaign that stirred support in Havana and abroad. The guerrillas' efforts ended in victory a little more than two years later.

Batista fled to exile in the Dominican Republic on New Year's Eve of 1958. He finally settled in and died a natural death in another dictatorship, Franco's Spain. Batista's choice of Spain was to become popular with other retired tyrants. Two ousted Latin American dictators, Juan D. Peron of Argentina and Marcos Perez Jimenez of Venezuela, eventually became comfortably ensconced in Madrid.

The first of Castro's forces reached Havana on January 2, 1959. Castro made his triumphant entry six days later and the next stage of the Cuban Revolution was underway.

Castro and Washington, however, got off to a bad start. The administration of President Dwight D. Eisenhower fanned speculation that Castro was a communist, a popular suspicion of many people during the Cold War. Other criticism of the Cuban Revolution bubbled up in the United States when Castro-appointed tribunals and began ordering the execution of Batista officials accused of torture and murder. The new Cuban government, especially Castro, reacted angrily to the criticism. There had been no outrage in the United States when Batista men killed dozens of political opponents without even considering trials, and Castro believed the entire issue was not the business of the United States anyway.

On a trip to the United States in April of 1959, Castro met with Vice President Richard Nixon (Eisenhower was conveniently out of town playing golf), who announced after a private talk with the Cuban leader that he was convinced Castro was controlled by communists. Less than a month later, Castro announced agrarian reform, a favorite Marxist program that turned large acreage owned by American companies over to peasants to farm.

On March 4, 1960, the French freighter La Coubre carrying munitions to Cuba from Belgium mysteriously exploded in Havana harbor, killing several Cubans. Castro was outraged and accused the United States of sabotage. U.S. Senate Intelligence Committee reports show that it was about this time that the CIA began its first moves to kill Castro. But Havana's regime was not idle either. It nationalized U.S.-owned sugar mills in Cuba. Che Guevara, Cuba's new industrial boss, advised British and American oil companies they would have to begin refining imported Soviet oil. Eisenhower cut Cuba's sugar quota.

In September 1960, Castro went to New York to attend the United Nations General Assembly, where he embraced Soviet Premier Nikita Khrushchev, publicly seeding a Cuba-Soviet alliance that was to last until Soviet communism failed 30 years later.

Two months after the Havana-Moscow embrace, John F. Kennedy won the presidency. But 18 days before Kennedy could be inaugurated in January 1961, Eisenhower broke diplomatic relations with Cuba. He left Kennedy with a secret CIA plan to invade Cuba.

Playa Giron, Cuba's name for the Bay of Pigs, failed almost before it started on April 17, 1961. Castro was aware that a U.S.-supported invasion by Cuban exiles was coming. His recently trained militia and army were in the right places as invaders came ashore in a swamp on Cuba's south coast. The Cuban leader's meager air force sank or routed the invaders' supply ships. Kennedy had withheld air power, and the ground fighting was over in two days. Castro took nearly 1,200 invaders prisoner, and Kennedy suffered the worst political setback of his career.

Eighteen months later, to Castro's anguish, Kennedy forced the Soviet Union and Premier Khrushchev to withdraw Soviet medium-range missiles, presumably with nuclear warheads, that Moscow had secretly installed in Cuba. The October 1962 confrontation risked nuclear war before Khrushchev backed down and ordered the missiles removed. Castro did not want a nuclear holocaust but he felt Cuba had been sold down the river by Cold War politics between Washington and Moscow. When I reached Havana, his irritation at Moscow's decision was evidenced by his continued attacks on Soviet trade with South American countries that opposed him and the Kremlin's refusal to support armed revolution outside Cuba's borders.

The AP had maintained a correspondent and an office in Havana after Castro came to power, and nobody from the world's then largest newsgathering organization had been expelled during Cuba's confrontations with the United States. So I began work, more immediately concerned about my fluency in Spanish than I was about Cuba's contribution to the Cold War or Castro. That concern was soon to be overtaken.

Chapter Five

PACO

Francisco Teira Alfonso told U.S. senators more than a year after both of us had left Cuba that my reply about being a journalist and not a judge "is what really made Castro angry and after that he tried to implicate Wheeler in anything damaging so he could be implicated as a spy ... . They really tried to destroy his personality."

Teira, according to the accounts he gave to the U.S. Senate Internal Security subcommittee after he defected from Cuba, was a former press officer for the Castro government who doubled as an intelligence agent. He was one of my earliest friends in Cuba. I was not the only person he fooled as he walked his political tightrope. He duped lovers and Cuban intelligence as well. Paco — the diminutive for Francisco — started out as a dedicated Castroite. He was an arms buyer and fund-raiser for Castro in Havana, New York, and Miami before Castro came to power.

Born and educated in the Cuban capital, he began his "revolutionary" life when he was 21, after being arrested for anti-Batista activities in 1954. He was lucky. A relative who was a physician in the fingerprint section of the Batista government's bureau of investigation heard about the arrest, intervened, and arranged for Paco's quick release. At the time, Paco was closest to the anti-Batista Authentic and Orthodox parties but not a member of either. Neither was he a member of Castro's 26th of July Movement. But after his arrest he was approached by a 26th of July leader, and he began, as he testified, "to cooperate by selling bonds and collecting funds for the organization. Then I started to cooperate in the collection of arms and transportation of people, people who were in danger, to find them a proper place to hide, and so I got involved with the 26th of July Movement."

He gained further favor with the Castro movement after he went to the United States in 1956, got a job at an insurance company in New York, and began raising money and arms for Castro's guerrilla war in the Sierra Maestra. He later went to Miami and did the same thing.

After Castro took over in Cuba in early 1959, Paco returned to Havana. For three months early in 1961 he went through a Marxist school that the revolutionary government had set up in the Vedado section of Havana at Paseo and 15th Street. The school was to train selected people for positions in the new government. According to him, classes ran 10 hours daily. This effort and training ended in April, one week after the Bay of Pigs and more than seven months before Castro was to confirm his communism publicly by declaring "I am a Marxist and have been one all my life."

Paco went into the Castro government early in 1964 and became the official foreign press contact man at the Cuban

Foreign Affairs Ministry, an important post, obviously held with Castro's approval. As such, Paco said he also worked for Cuban intelligence and eventually counter-intelligence.

By the mid-1960s, however, he was beginning to lose his revolutionary fervor. He fell into disfavor, some of it real, some of it officially devised. By the time I met him in 1967, he had lost his foreign ministry job and was a manager-trainee in the Cuban shipping company. He became a purser in 1968 for the company Lineas Mambisas, traveling to several foreign countries, including China, where he was arrested after taking pictures of the Shanghai River. Chinese authorities checked his record, learned he had been in Cuban intelligence, and concluded he was spying on China on behalf of the Soviet Union. He was not, but Chinese authorities forced a written confession from him to that effect in return for letting him go free and returning to his ship. He jumped ship in the Panama Canal on August 20, 1969, and asked for political asylum in the United States. He left a divorced wife and two children in Havana.

On February 24 and 25, 1971, Paco testified to his personal and political history before Sen. James Eastland's Internal Security subcommittee. Although it appears that, at times in his testimony, Paco was courting Senate favor or paying for his admission to the United States with information, his testimony is nonetheless revealing. It gave me a shiver when I first read it and still does after all these years. This is some of his direct testimony:

We used to bug the rooms with electronic devices and things like that. This was the modus operandi with the journalists, and I can say that we used the same method with the personnel of the foreign embassies and the foreign press agencies in Cuba, especially those of the Western countries like AP, UPI and Reuters. ...

After I was terminated from my job (near the end of 1966) in the Foreign Affairs Ministry, I was ordered by the Department of Security of the State (DSE) to continue my contacts with these people who believed that they were close to me and they thought that we were on friendly terms. ...

I was informed by the DSE that now I had an opportunity to get with them on friendlier terms and that I could even pretend to be a dissenter to be on the subversive side. I was also ordered to try to do things in a more secretive way, telling them that I could not be seen with them in public places so they would gather the impression that I opposed the regime, that I was a subversive.

Of course this plan had been conceived for the purpose of misleading them to a point where proof could be gathered that they were working as agents of the U.S. government.

This was the case with the Associated Press man. There was no problem with UPI because the bureau chief was a Cuban national, and they knew for a long time that he was in their hands. He was a very careful man, very careful with what he reported.

It was different with the AP man. They were really trying to get him involved. And it was very hard for me because I did not want to lend myself to a machination that would have damaged an individual, especially an individual for whom I felt real friendship. It was very hard for me to keep him out of trouble because I had to play the role of double agent and I had to report his activities.

He never tried to recruit me, but sometimes he would engage me in certain kinds of conversation that I felt I had to report to the DSE, for fear that he might have informed this to some of the mentioned (Cuban) double agents. You see I was forced to do that to protect myself. My reports were noncommittal because I would say that I saw him and he was very reserved in his conversations with me.

I found myself in the middle because, at the time, the Cuban government, and specifically Fidel Castro himself, was very much interested in proving that the man was a CIA agent or at least that he had been co-opted by the CIA. Actually, Fidel wanted to involve the Associated Press office in Havana in a scandal of being a nest of espionage agents for propaganda purposes and to make it lose prestige in the eyes of the Americans and give proof to the world that the United States was using all means to infiltrate agents in Cuba.

Fidel Castro was very interested in concocting such a scandal. The DSE had tried to involve Ike Flores (previous AP correspondent), but the man did not fit their requirements. According to their plan, they singled out John Wheeler of AP as the perfect target for this purpose.

I don't know why, but John Wheeler used to make Castro real mad. He was a man who could really provoke anger in Castro. On the other hand, Castro would characterize him as the typical American imperialist, a good cadre of American imperialism. Don't ask me why, but Castro could not be around other journalists if John Wheeler was among them. Despite the fact that he had made him angry, at the same time he recognized the fact that John Wheeler was a smart man.

What really made him (Castro) angry was during an appearance when he was trying to salvage the fiasco resulting from the OLAS conference. On this occasion he (Castro) paraded some alleged counterrevolutionary agents and weapons captured on the north shore of Cuba. President Dorticós asked Wheeler whether he was satisfied that there was enough proof to indict the United States for this operation.

It was my reply, Paco testified, that so angered Castro that "they really tried to charge him with CIA charges; and it was a little bit difficult because, actually, he was not an agent. He was a correspondent, and, as I could approach him myself, I was convinced that he was just a journalist."

Repeatedly I was told 'well Paco this time you have got to do your best to prove this man is a CIA agent,' and well this was very sarcastic, you see it was ordered to me in a very sarcastic way, that if he is not, you make him a CIA agent.

I was ordered this by Andres, who worked directly under (Carlos) Neira. He was the officer of the DSE in charge of the coordination with all the press. His real name was Raul Pujol.

Then Senate chief investigator Alfonso Tarabochia asked: "They wanted to frame him?"

Paco: "They wanted to frame Wheeler, yes."
Tarabochia: "To appear as a spy for the CIA?"
Paco: "That is right."
Tarabochia: "But were they successful?"

Paco: "They were not successful. First, I was protecting him most of the time, and second, they tried many approaches to frame him, but I would warn him about some of them. In the end he knew I was really disgusted with the regime. I had a certain amount of sympathy for him. I did not dare tell him that that was actually the objective of security. I told him he had to be very careful with people to whom he talked to, not to trust anyone, even if he thought that he was recruiting an informer, and not dare to recruit anyone because I let him know that they wanted to make it appear the government was trying to make it appear that he was a master spy.

"To not try to say anything to anybody, no matter how much confidence he thought he had in this man whom he thought his friend, he should not believe that he had any friends there but himself and he should start saying to everybody that I was a member of DSE and that I was trying to approach him and things like that. So I would report myself to security that I was not having further success with this job with Wheeler and I could get away from this assignment."

Paco was asked by Tarabochia about journalists approved by the Castro government to attend the 1967 OLAS conference and if any of them had been "co-opted by the Cuban intelligence apparatus." Paco answered with five names. One surprised me when I read the testimony. But it answered a question I had often pondered. The name as Paco gave it was "Marta Solis. She was married to a Cuban national and worked for the Cuban intelligence too." Her role two years after the OLAS conference would confirm Paco's words just as I was being thrown out of the country.

I met Paco Teira about two months after I arrived in Cuba. I had been put in touch with him by the Reuters correspondent, who told me Paco had lost his job at the Foreign Affairs Ministry at the end of 1966 because his high-living and playboy antics clashed with the Revolution's image and with its politics. A Western diplomat seconded that information but said Paco still was well-informed and could be "useful."

So I took Paco to lunch at one of the few restaurants reserved for foreigners with hard currency and where they had most everything that was listed on the menu. I think it was the 1830 Restaurant. Paco seemed to enjoy a brief return to his old life style and ate everything on his plate. He also seemed genuinely glad to see an American in Havana who wasn't connected to the Cuban government. I was told there were about 100 of them in Cuba at the time. I eventually met a few of them. One was Lionel Martin, who worked for the Cuban news agency Prensa Latina and had been in Cuba since Eisenhower broke relations with Havana. Martin later did an informative book on Castro's life as a young man. I had only fleeting contact with him. But I remember well an American couple who were campaigning to trade their Cuban residency for life in East Germany. I thought they had been too long in the sun.

Paco's English (he also spoke Italian) was first class, and he certainly looked like he could be a *bon vivant*. He was handsome enough to be a stand-in for Rock Hudson — tall, big-shouldered, and a full head of dark hair. He was well informed on Castro history, forthright in answering questions, and entertaining. One of his first questions to me was if I knew the American correspondent (now a columnist and author) Georgie Anne Geyer. She had interviewed Castro in Cuba in 1966 when Paco was head of the foreign press section. I heard Paco had an affair with her (correspondents' gossip), but I told him I did not know her and he let the matter drop. In her book "Buying the Night Flight," Geyer mentions a brief love affair with a broad-shouldered Cuban named "Paco."

In testimony before the Senate Internal Security subcommittee after he defected, Paco mentioned a handful of American journalists who had been given "the treatment" during their visits to Cuba. The treatment was basically deception, he said. If the journalist refused government transportation and preferred a taxi, he or she got one. But the cab driver was a security "plant." If they wanted to interview an ordinary Cuban, there was another plant. The treatment also included electronic surveillance and, if the journalist desired, a sexual partner.

The treatment and its ancillary efforts, of course, did not always work. Sometimes it backfired. One case I knew of involved Bert Quint of CBS-TV, who was named by Paco in his testimony as one of those targeted for the treatment while Paco was still in the foreign ministry. Quint may have been giving Paco a kind of treatment, too.

In post-Paco times, Quint came to my office to chat at the end of a brief assignment to ask if by chance I knew of any unused TV film anywhere. He said the foreign ministry had advised him it wanted to take his film and review it. If it was approved, the ministry said it would send it on to him in the United States, I suppose via Canada. There were, in fact, a couple of cans of old unused film in an office cabinet. Stanley said they had been left by another American crew, perhaps NBC. Quint took them, and I presume used them to satisfy the foreign ministry's request. Officials must have been surprised when they developed them.

Paco's testimony before the Senate subcommittee showed he also was involved in giving the treatment to diplomats. J.G. Sourwine, chief counsel for the subcommittee, elicited testimony to that effect with this question: "Now what connection, if any, did you have with the Directorate General of Intelligence? (DGI)"

> Paco: "I had assignments from the security department to mingle as much as possible with the diplomatic personnel not at the level of the ambassadors or counselors but just with the secondary level personnel, let us say first secretaries and second secretaries ... I was told to play the role of playboy because of my physical appearance and ability to attract women. I used to practice several sports — I had a plane, a sports car, a yacht, practiced sky diving, judo, polo, and all this was facilitated by the DGI in order to give the necessary image to accomplish my given role ... . Security wanted to give me such a facade so that the diplomats could come to me because I was someone to talk to. ... I was different because, first, I had been here in the United States for several years and was very Western myself to start with; so if I was good at it, it was because I was natural at it."

> Sourwine: "Did you ever get an assignment which required you to make love to a woman in order to achieve some purpose of state security?"

> Paco: "Yes, many times."

One afternoon Paco surprised me by coming to my office, and, after we had talked about nothing important on the steps outside the office, he suddenly told me I was being watched and to be very careful in everything I did and said. I asked him whether I was being followed. "They know every movement you make. You are being tracked everywhere," he said.

Several weeks later he surprised me again, this time by asking whether he would have to talk to the CIA if he went to the United States. I said I had no idea and frankly did not want to talk about it. I told him I wasn't certain he would have to talk to the CIA but that whomever he talked with probably would be linked directly to the CIA, if not a CIA agent themselves. He also told me that he had tried to leave Cuba in a small boat but had been spotted by a Cuban coastal patrol plane as he approached the 12-mile limit. He told me he damaged the outboard engine so that he could tell the patrol he had been fishing and was drifting helplessly when they caught up with him. I told him again I didn't want to know anything about what happened or what he was planning if anything. He nodded in agreement, shook my hand, and left.

I lost touch with Paco in the summer of 1969 and heard he was aboard a Mambisa ship. Later, a secretary at the Indian Embassy in Havana pulled me aside at a diplomatic reception and worriedly told me that she had not heard from him for weeks.

I never saw Paco again.

Che Guevara, Raul Castro and Fidel Castro

Chapter Six

CHE

Two months, more or less, after Fidel Castro publicly chastised me, one of the few American journalists he trusted was sitting in my office. Herbert Matthews, a man to whom Castro's door was almost always open, had dropped by a couple of days before. But this October night he had come to the Havana AP office to watch Castro announce to the nation that Ernesto "Che" Guevara was dead. He had been killed while trying to start a Cuban-style revolution in Boliva

Matthews either didn't know or didn't care whether I was in disfavor. I hadn't said anything to him about it because I didn't think it mattered so much any more. I now reckoned that I might be crawling my way out of Castro's dog house. One reason for this was that 48 hours earlier I had received a call from the Cuban Foreign Ministry asking that any available AP wire photos from Bolivia showing Guevara's body be sent to it as soon as possible. The ministry had asked the same of the UPI. A ministry official said Castro wanted to confirm absolutely that Guevara was dead before he said anything to the country. Castro might not trust *Yanqui* words, but he apparently felt he could rely on *Yanqui* pictures.

Our office sent the ministry all we had. The one I remember best showed Che lifeless on a slab. He sure looked dead. Matthews and I sat, mostly silent, both of us intent on watching a somber Castro on the AP's snowy black and white television set. It was the same one on which I had seen El Maximo Lider denounce me.

Yes, Che had been slain, Castro said, fighting to hold his own emotions in control when he said it. He then began a speech that Matthew was to describe later in his book, *Revolution in Cuba,* as one of the Cuban leader's most moving. Matthew's eyes were misty as he watched and listened to Castro. I, too, thought it was a helluva speech.

Matthews had come to Cuba to gather material for his latest book, which was his second on Castro and the Cuban revolution. He had earned Castro's respect and trust in 1957, when, as a Latin American expert and reporter for *The New York Times*, he had gone secretly to the Sierra Maestra and found Castro and his band of rebels still alive and armed after Batista's government had announced Castro and his men had been killed. Matthews' reporting was later blamed by some anti-Castroites in the United States for helping Castro to power, and he was often accused by exiles in Miami of being an apologist for Cuba's communist regime.

Castro's confirmation of Guevara's death visibly touched Matthews, and many Cubans as well. Perhaps, listening to the Cuban leader speak that night, it seemed fateful to Matthews that he would hear Castro announce Che's death when Matthews was in Havana not in the United States. For Guevara was no stranger to the reporter. Che had been among the depleted ranks of Castro's rebel army 10 years earlier, when Matthews had met them in the mountains of Eastern Cuba. He knew Che's story well.

Castro's speech was the first announcement to the nation of where Che had been and what he had been doing since he had disappeared from Cuba. Guevara's exact whereabouts in Bolivia had been known only to Castro and a few high-ranking Cuban officials. But there were earlier signs that Guevara's location was being bracketed like an artillery target. In his Bolivian diary, Che noted at the end of April that — with Havana's publication earlier that month of Che's call for creating other Vietnams — "there can be no doubt about my presence here (in Bolivia)."

At the end of June, Bolivian president Rene Barrientos told a news conference that Guevara was in Bolivia and would be captured soon. A *New York Times* story on July 29 said "Cuban-inspired" guerrillas had been sighted four months earlier in the Nacahuazu Valley, 420 miles southeast of La Paz, the Bolivian capital.

In early August 1967, an AP story from La Paz said a woman guerrilla, code-named Taniawas, used a bullhorn in the Nacahuazu Valley to urge Bolivian soldiers to surrender to Guevara's guerrillas. The AP story described her activity as a jungle version of World War II's Tokyo Rose, whose broadcasts urged American servicemen to surrender to the Japanese. The Argentine-born Tania , whose real name was Haydee Tamara Bunke, was trained in Cuba and sent to Bolivia months before Guevara got there. Her job was to prepare support for Guevara's arrival. She joined one of his bands of rebels after Guevara moved into the jungles of Bolivia and was said to be a close friend of his. Tania was killed by Bolivian troops 21 days after the pro-revolution conference in Havana that had named Guevara as its honorary chairman. Contact between Guevara and Havana was probably sporadic at best when Castro had made his speech closing that conference.

On October 8, 1967, Guevara was wounded and captured. His tired, struggling band of Cuban guerrillas was wiped out by Bolivian Rangers, who were being aided and directed by the CIA. According to Cuban accounts, Guevara was executed the next day by a drunken Bolivian sergeant.

About nine months after Castro's speech announcing Guevara's death, the Cuban government scored a political and publishing coup. It said it had obtained photocopies of Guevara's diary, detailing his 11-month effort to try to foment a revolution in Bolivia. The government gave no clues as to how it got the copies but said no money had changed hands to get them. Castro said Che's handwritten record of the guerrilla campaign would also be published in West Germany, France, Italy, Spain, Chile, Mexico, and in the United States by *Ramparts* magazine.

Almost immediately, Bolivian President Barrientos (regularly dubbed a gorilla by the Cuban press) declared the diary published by the Cubans was a fraud. Barrientos himself was reported to have hoped to sell the diary for at least $100,000, but someone in his government later identified as Interior minister Antonio Arguedas reportedly got so fed up with CIA pressure in the case that he secretly sent microfilms of the diary to the Castro government.

Castro was furious about Barrientos' accusation that the diary was not authentic. On July 3, 1968, he spoke to the

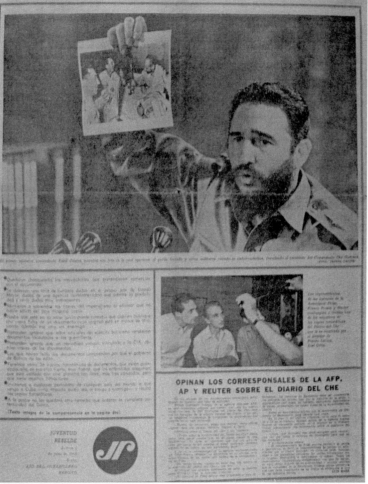

Headline says Fidel Castro accuses Bolivian President Rene Barrientos of lying about the diary of Che Guevara. The bottom of the newspaper quotes opinion of AP reporter Wheeler (far left) on the diary's authenticity.

nation on television saying the Bolivian leaders were liars and that Cuba had proven the authenticity of the diary. He said that although the original diary was in the hands of the "imperialists," they had not made it public because they were afraid it could bulwark support for Guevara's ideas and principles. Castro noted that the CIA had copies of the diary and had given it to selected Western journalists in Bolivia. He showed his anger by displaying before the television cameras a photograph of Bolivian General Alfredo Ovando and two other military men drinking and celebrating the death of Guevara.

Copies of the Cuban publication of Guervara's diary were promptly delivered to foreign journalists in Havana, and Castro said any journalist in the world who wanted a free copy was welcome to come to Cuba and get one and then compare it with the diary the Bolivians had. The next day the communist youth newspaper, *Juventud Rebelde* interviewed me and the correspondents of Reuters and Agence France Presse about our views on the authenticity, then front-paged our answers. I was again being called on to be a judge, but I was ready this time. I typed this out for the newspaper: "The majority, no much more than a majority of the people and diplomats with whom I have talked, including diplomats of Western countries, have no doubt as to the authenticity of the diary." Mindful of how the same newspaper had scalded me before, I made an extra copy of what I had written. My judgment this time passed muster.

To this day, Che's diary remains fascinating reading to followers of the Cuban Revolution and Che's style of guerrilla warfare. But it was not popular with the Soviet

Union when Castro announced its publication, and it was notable that Castro had not mentioned whether the diary would be reproduced in the Soviet Union or the Soviet-controlled East Bloc. The Warsaw Pact nations, of course, generally hewed to the Soviet position against fomenting revolution by armed struggle. Guevara's failure to succeed in Bolivia seemed to sanctify that Soviet stance. Besides, Castro and Moscow had been fussing openly for months. Castro's promotion of the diary and the Soviet bloc's reaction to it were probably to be expected.

In his defense of the diary's genuineness, Castro made an interesting remark. The remark became an inadvertent harbinger of an event that, less than two months later, was to surprise a lot of people on both sides of communism: The Soviet Union's invasion of Czechoslovakia and the end of "the Prague Spring." Castro noted in his television address on the Guevara diary that the official Czech news agency, CTK, had cast doubts on the diary's authenticity. "In Czechoslovakia there presently is great freedom of the press," he said, making such a liberty sound like a contagious disease that needed to be stamped out as soon as possible. He added that Cuba did not question the Czech news agency's right to doubt the diary was genuine, but he suggested that, because the CTK news dispatch doing so had a Washington dateline, the Czech reporter had been "influenced by the atmosphere" in the U.S. capital.

The publication of the diary quickly aroused strange new speculation by some Western embassies in Havana about a significant change in Cuban-Soviet relations. Castro had decided to abandon exporting revolution from Cuba and was giving in to the Soviet position, so the speculation went, because the diary showed how Guevara's mission of armed revolution had failed. Henceforth, Castro would support revolution outside of Cuba only if it were home grown. Over the years that theory now seems close to correct. But at the time, I could not risk "storifying" that theory as it was presented. I limited my reporting to saying that Guevara's death had been at least a temporary setback for Cuban revolutionary ventures. I didn't even consider interviewing Guevara's widow in Havana, Aleida March, who had confirmed the authenticity of the handwriting in Guevara's diary. For one thing, I didn't think she would see me, let alone talk to me. And, knowing Castro's strong attachment for Guevara, I also felt such a move would have meant a quick forced exit for me from Cuba. Covering the news was more restrained and less intrusive in those days, especially so from inside Cuba.

Chapter Seven

A LONE RANGER

To get most Americans interested in foreign news, you have to hit them over the head with a war or a natural disaster, either of which have to involve Americans. The foreign news audience invariably dwindles in proportion to the number of Americans involved. It has been reported over and over again that people in the United States know and care less about foreign affairs than most Europeans, many Asians, and lots of Latin Americans. Sometimes the messenger is blamed, as was often the case in the Vietnam War, when the news was bad. But people griping about the U.S. press usually confine their complaints to domestic news, not the reports from abroad. And few bother to worry about how anybody abroad gathers foreign news.

After many months in Havana, I, too, was still wondering how to do it. A feeling persisted that I often came up with less than half the story. This was bothersome, but not too surprising, I suppose, considering I was a one-man band trying to orchestrate the AP news from Havana. In the Soviet Union during the Cold War days, most foreign correspondents were confined to Moscow, usually restricted to living in compounds assigned to foreigners and seldom if ever allowed to travel unescorted from the capital. But that was not my situation. If I had enough gasoline, I could travel out of Havana any time I wanted and go any where I wanted, except near the U.S. Guantanamo Naval Base at the eastern end of the island. That restriction was self-imposed. But I applied it to all military installations in Cuba.

One hitch, of course, was that I was the only journalist covering and writing the news for the AP. If something newsworthy happened when I was out of the capital, there would be nobody to report it. Working for a news agency, such a gaffe could be professionally fatal. Newspapers, even networks, can miss stories. News agencies cannot. Besides, news of most countries develops in the capital, and that's the place to be. This was vitally true in Cuba. Havana was my only communications link with the AP. Anywhere else I would probably be out of luck.

There were several stories I always wanted to do but never had the chance because I had to stick close to Havana. One was to follow Castro's guerrilla trail in Oriente Province, and see how the Revolution had changed life along its borders. Another was to accompany any of the visiting American student brigades when they went to work in Cuba's agriculture. I would also have liked to talk to people on both ends of the island about an old story, the 1962 missile crisis. With a controlled press, how much did they know about it? Everything? Half of it? At one time I considered trying to go to Guantanamo to see if fences reportedly put up by both the United States and Cuba around the U.S. Navy base with a no man's land between them would qualify as a Caribbean version of the Berlin Wall. Some Cuban film I had seen showed U.S. Marines clowning around on their side of the U.S. fence and making obscene gestures. I wondered if the Cuban side sometimes replied. But I abandoned the idea of a story when I realized the AP would want photos, and trying to get close enough to take them would surely land me in the hands of Cuban security.

One goal I hoped to accomplish was to show the Cuban government and Castro that I was not in any way connected with the U.S. government. I think I finally convinced some people nearest to Castro that I was neither in Washington's pay nor its debt. But many others, both inside and outside of his government, continued to believe that I was somehow linked to the government of my country. Any Cuban journalist working abroad would of course not only be aligned with, but working for the Cuban government. It seemed only logical for many Cubans to presume the same of me. Besides, Castro had branded me with a cadre connection, and everybody in revolutionary Cuba knew that meant I was on a team, in my case this meant some kind of U.S. government team.

Truth be told, I am certain now that I was dancing in and out, mostly out, of favor with Castro. In a country where one man is the final and only authority, it's not good to step on his toes and be a Yankee, to boot. So the TV newsreel and still cameras kept focusing on me at Castro speeches, particularly when the front-row revolutionaries led the shouts encouraging him to "hit the Yankees hard." Or when Castro denounced "U.S. aggression in Vietnam."

One of the crowd favorites that turned the lights on me was for Castro or almost any speaker to denounce "imperialism's economic blockade" of "our Cuba." Just the word imperialism seemed to direct a lot of attention my way. As the cameras whirred (and in Cuba in those days they really were noisy), I was driven to develop a defense. It turned out to be something like this: I didn't look up at the cameras and I wrote furiously in my notebook as if I were recording every word to send back to the United States. More likely I scribbled something like "the quick brown fox jumped over the lazy dog's etc.," or the start of Lincoln's Gettysburg address. If I was feeling somewhat set upon, I sometimes wrote, in Spanish, "*dale duro a los Yanquis*" ("hit the Yankees hard").

When Castro said something newsworthy during those moments, I occasionally missed part of it. I usually got it back later from other correspondents. Most were willing to help. More than a few of them, mostly from the East Bloc, also thought I could speak for Washington. I recall in particular being asked more than once what my reaction was (meaning the U.S. government's) to the 1968 Tet offensive in Vietnam, which stunned and set back the American military. The Cold War was always present, and when the Cuban press needed a Western response and, above all, a U.S. response, reporters came to me with questions.

Every other foreign correspondent in Cuba had an embassy to get information from or to go to bat for them. But I was a journalistic "Lone Ranger," isolated, working for a news agency headquartered in enemy territory and already identified nationally as anti-Cuban by Havana's leader. I was the nearest thing to Tio Sam the Cubans had. I was a political leper.

Despite the officially declared hatred for the Yankee colossus to the north of Cuba, I never heard an uncivil word directed at me during the demonstrations of anti-U.S. feelings. Nor did any member of the Cuban press ever show anything but professional courtesy during those times.

Security was a different matter. I suppose I was followed more than I suspected. But with traffic normally being light in Havana, and with no morning or evening rush hours to restrict vision, I felt I could see most of what was behind and in front of me. Most people walked, bicycled or traveled aboard one of the crowded British Leyland buses that traversed the capital's streets. Few Cubans had operating cars or the fuel to power them. It seemed logical under those circumstances to believe it would be easy to see if you were being followed. Chauffeur Esmond Grant seemed to see spooks at every stop sign. Sometimes I thought I did. Taxis, if their drivers were young, could arouse suspicions. But much of the time it was the surveillance covering government buildings and entities or foreign embassies that told Cuban state security where I was and how long I stayed there. There was also surveillance from neighborhood watch groups. I don't think any other foreign journalist even approached the level of surveillance leveled on me.

Despite the uneasy feeling of being watched, I seldom felt I needed protection. If I had, I would have been dependent on the Swiss Embassy, which was charged with representing what few U.S. interests remained in Cuba. The Swiss also represented ten other countries without diplomatic status in Havana. Most of those were Latin American nations heeding the Organization of American States (OAS) ouster from its ranks of Castro's Cuba. Mexico ignored the OAS ban and maintained diplomatic relations with Cuba. In the Havana of those days, the only Spanish-speaking embassy besides Mexico belonged to Spain. To me, the Swiss diplomats always seemed very comfortable in reinforcing their reputation as professional neutrals. As far as I was personally concerned, they were useless. I operated with the belief that as long as I was doing my job and not doing anything that could be considered counterrevolutionary, I would not need any protection, diplomatic or otherwise. It was one of my assessments, thank goodness, that proved correct.

Beneath those surface feelings, however, I was always a bit nervous about being watched and judged. I was careful with both written and spoken words. I addressed people, official or otherwise, as *companero* or *companera*, the terms Cubans used instead of "comrade." I tried to fit in just a little to demonstrate I had no anti-Cuban feelings or devious motives. But I was always conscious that the wrong words could mean expulsion. Could a journalist have had a better job? Or a lonelier one?

At the start of my time in Cuba, I had naively hoped to demonstrate my neutrality with news coverage. But as time went by, I knew I was unlikely to succeed. I was battling a history, old and new, of bad feelings between the United States and Cuba. The Cold War had widened that political gulf between the two countries. Although Moscow and Vietnam were thousands of miles from Cuba, both seemed much closer than that in Havana. Nobody there in those days, it seemed, could be considered neutral.

Still I tried. In our first days in Cuba, Ann and I went one Sunday to the Havana Yacht Club. I was interested to see how one of the centerpieces of the Batista dictatorship had changed.

The portly cigar smokers in their blazers and yachting caps that I had read about in years past were no where in sight. Instead, we were surrounded by a group of 20 young people as we sat down at an empty veranda table, knowing there would be no food, perhaps no drink. However, there was Son the Revolution's version of Coca Cola. The secret formula to that world-famous U.S. product had been destroyed by the parent company in capitalism's last Cuban hours. And the Cuban substitute, frankly, was lousy. But we drank it as the young people, most of them in their early teens, and their skin color ranging from white to black began asking us questions.

"Where are you from?" asked a tall slender boy. I remember they were all slender. "We are North Americans," I said, aware that many people south of the Rio Grande dislike the U.S. custom of monopolizing the word "American."

"From Canada then?"

"No, from the United States," I replied.

"So you are working for the Revolution," said another youth approvingly.

"I am a foreign correspondent," I said.

"What's that?" asked a girl. Somebody else asked if we were imperialists.

I tried to explain our presence in Cuba. I said I worked for the AP. None of the teens seemed to know what the AP was. I liked that. So I said that in working as a correspondent. I wrote about what Fidel Castro said and did. That was taken with general approval.

"Do you have any Beatle records?" said a voice from the back.

"Why does the United States continue to blockade Cuba?" interrupted an older youth.

I gulped down the last of the bad cola, said we had no Beatles records, and answered that I didn't know why the economic boycott of Cuba by the United States continued. I still don't today. But I do know that journalism hasn't been to blame for it.

SUDDEN COMMUNISM

Life for me in Cuba, for whatever reasons, felt less tense at the start of 1968. Ann was taking guitar lessons, singing old street vendor songs and Cuban lullabies, learning about Havana. We had made some friends. I began thinking and talking about Castro as "Fidel," what all Cubans called him. I thought I was getting the hang of reporting from behind the so-called bamboo curtain. As it turned out, I would need to be very deft at that. Cuba was going to be full of bad news in the year that lay ahead.

Officially, it was designated the "Year of the Heroic Guerrilla," in tribute to the slain Guevara. Nineteen sixty-eight, however, did not start well. Fidel Castro, in his annual state-of-the-revolution speech on January 2, announced the country was going to have gasoline rationing. The reason was that the Soviet Union had turned down Cuba's request for an increase in the oil Moscow supplied to Havana. Dependent almost exclusively on Soviet oil, Cuba had asked for an increase in petroleum deliveries to match its projected industrial and agricultural growth. Castro told the audience massed to hear him and already struggling with food and

Sugar cane harvest in early 1960s

clothing rationing that it was beneath the dignity of the
Cuban revolution to beg the Soviets for more oil, a clear dig
at what he felt were Moscow's miserly methods.

That was not a nice thing for one socialist brother to say
to the other, especially in public. Despite Soviet financial aid

averaging one million dollars daily, Cuba considered Moscow a brother, not a parent. "We don't have a father," declared Raul Castro, Fidel's younger brother by five years and the No. 2 man in Cuba. This was after a cool visit to Havana by Soviet Premier Aleksei Kosygin. Cuban-Soviet relations, Raul Castro said, were based on "strict mutual respect and absolute independence." But Cuba produced little or no petroleum of its own. It was dependent on the Soviet Union for almost every barrel it consumed.

The Soviet stance on oil for Cuba reflected one of several continuing conflicts between Moscow and Havana. Castro was still miffed about Premier Nikita Khrushchev's removal of Soviet missiles from Cuba in the showdown with President John F. Kennedy nearly six years earlier. When Kosygin, Krushchev's successor as premier, visited Havana ahead of the OLAS meeting, he got a polite but restrained reception. Castro began openly criticizing the Soviet Union for doing business with what he considered reactionary Latin governments.

Castro also had a basic disagreement with the Soviet Union's position of not supporting revolutionary movements, especially in South America. He attacked the Soviet-beholden Communist Party in Venezuela and later the Moscow-line communist parties in Colombia and Bolivia. He said Bolivian communist leaders, by their ineptitude and lack of support, had in effect betrayed Guevara and helped cause his capture.

East Bloc journalists in Havana and one Soviet had indicated to me in conversations more than once that they felt Castro should concentrate more on the economy and less on guerrilla warfare. Near the end of a six-hour speech on March 13, the anniversary of an attack by Havana University students on Batista's palace, Castro said he was going to do just that. He announced the government was going to put an end to all private businesses still operating in Cuba. His announcement woke up the crowd of thousands gathered at the university, some of whom had been fighting sleep as Castro spoke into the early morning hours of the next day. The entire nation was to get a much bigger awakening in the months and years ahead.

With gasoline rationing barely two months old, nationalization came as a new hardship, one that changed life in Cuba for everyone. Three days later, on a Saturday night, the bars and night clubs didn't open as usual. Soldiers, militia members, and some members of the Committees for the Defense of the Revolution (CDR) suddenly started turning crowds of surprised customers away, saying only that they were acting on government orders.

Six months earlier, I had written a story noting how life in Havana glittered compared to country living, where many families still had only bohios (thatch huts), no electricity, no water or other utilities, and were living like they had for years before Castro. In the capital, however, the young poured into Havana's streets at night. The bars were crowded, and rock 'n' roll mixed with Afro-Cuban rhythm. The night clubs presented big band music as if they were still in the '40s and splashy Las Vegas style shows. At the Tropicana night club, where all distinguished visitors of the Revolution inevitably showed up, chorines descended onto the stage from trees. There was a bongo beat and rum. It was, so I was told, almost like the old days.

But now the night life was gone, as well as all private business remaining in Cuba. Everything had been nationalized, everything but small farmers and their little acreage plots.

In all, more than 58,000 small businesses, from buses to bakeries, were seized and turned over to party leaders and many of the 2.4 million members of the CDR to manage. The takeover was called a "revolutionary offensive" aimed at "tearing capitalism out by the roots." Bank accounts of small business owners were frozen and proprietors allowed a maximum withdrawal of $200.

The government organized marching in the streets. The participants shouted "to death with capitalism and parasitism." Beards and long hair became unofficially unwelcome at the Castro alumnus the University of Havana. Boys in tight pants were denounced as vagrants and loafers. One principal target was the private grocery, sometimes an outlet for black marketeering. The government clamped new restrictions on milk, eggs, sugar, and crackers. Only bread could be bought in unlimited quantities. It, too, eventually fell under the anti-captialism knife. The nationalization also abolished the lottery and cockfighting, two hangovers that had lasted through nine years of Castro's revolution. Cockfighting had been a popular pastime in the Oriente Province, where Castro grew up.

Years later, Castro was to acknowledge that nationalization had been a mistake, too big of a step at the time, but anyone who suggested that in the spring of 1968 would have been considered a counterrevolutionary — an accusation that, if proven, often led to imprisonment. Six months after nationalization, I wrote that it had compounded the island's chronic shortage of consumer goods by wrapping it in red tape. It now took longer to get shoes repaired or get a haircut, and to do so you needed a "turn," or, in some cases, to fill out a form. The most common words on the street as queues for almost everything grew and grew became "*quien es el ultimo?*" —who's the last person in line? It is a phrase that has been etched in the history of the Revolution.

Employees in the AP office reflected the problem, especially the food shortages. Like the mass of Cubans, they were hungry for something besides eggs, and needed a new shirt and the detergent to wash it. As a foreign correspondent, however, I was in a special class. Along with the diplomats and some government officials, I had special privileges. We foreigners, for example, could dine at hard currency restaurants without waiting in line. We could also shop at a special government food store, where there were many things to eat and drink and household goods not available to the average Cuban. I have forgotten the full name of the store, known among its privileged shoppers simply by the part of its name that meant "the enterprise," in Spanish "*the empresa.*" The Soviets loved the *empresa* and their privileged status in being able to shop there. It was a real battle to beat them to the store each week when supplies arrived — before they grabbed up all the potatoes or fruit. After nationalization, Grant began chauffeuring Ann to the *empresa* once a week. She had extra time. Her guitar teacher had been gobbled up by the nationalization. At the *empresa*, Ann would help Grant fill his old Cadillac with as much food as seemed defensible, but never anything like the amounts some of the diplomats' cars carted off. On their return to the AP office, the food would be distributed equally among the employees. The staff members said they would be glad to reimburse the AP for the food in Cuban pesos. I refused the offer. We were swimming in pesos from distributing AP news and photos in Cuba. I have no idea how AP accounting in New York looked at this procedure when it finally was reported. But nobody in the AP organization ever complained about how much the Havana office spent on food or why.

The Castro government, meanwhile, said people made jobless by the nationalization would be given the equivalent of $50 to live on for one month if the government was not immediately able to place them in "productive work." The work the government had in mind was mostly agricultural, much of it designed to help meet Castro's earlier announced goal of a record 10 million tons of sugar production in 1970. If accomplished, it would surpass any sugar production achieved under capitalism. Cuba's sugar yield in 1967 was estimated at 6.1 million tons, well below the target of 7.5 million tons.

The programmed yield for 1968 was also running behind, due mostly to a drought and was expected to end up at 5.5 million tons, almost 3 million tons below the goal. Castro fearlessly declared the 10 million-ton goal would be "a yardstick by which to judge the capability of the

Revolution." He had first announced the plan in 1963, five years ahead of nationalization.

Another goal of the government's "revolutionary offensive" was to make Cuba the first truly communist country in the world. This meant creating what Castro termed "the new communist man." It was understood, of course, that this meant women, too. Women had, from the start, played key roles in Castro's rise to power. Castro's model of the new communist person would be a selfless, tireless worker who sweated for Cuba in order to build a moneyless society where all would share equally a new version of the old communist formula: from each according to his ability, to each according to his needs. Castro said Cuba's Revolution eventually would evolve to a state where money would be unnecessary. But first communist awareness had to be developed, he said. He already had equalized poverty. Hardship was next.

A good start would be to follow Che Guevara's call to be motivated by moral, not material, incentives. The government had already begun moving in that direction by ending material rewards such as home appliances or resort weekends for outstanding performances by workers in the cooperatives or the cane fields. In the future they would be declared "Heroes of the Revolution" instead. Renouncing overtime pay was recommended. So was volunteering. Absenteeism from the job and slacking off were shameful and anti-revolutionary.

Castro also had words for the Soviet Union — words that did little to hide his disappointment and, at times, disgust with the Russians for not pitching in with more aid. He seemed, in fact, to be accusing them of pressuring Cuba economically to change its revolutionary line. "We have known the bitterness of having to depend to a considerable extent on what we can get from abroad and have seen how this can be turned into a weapon — how, at the very least, there is a temptation to use it against our country," he said. Before nationalization, Castro had described his Revolution as having four stages: years of ignorance, years of agony, years of intense labor, and years of triumph. It soon became evident, however, that the second and third stages were to last a long time. And the fourth stage was not yet on the horizon.

On May 19, 1970, Castro acknowledged for the first time that the country would not reach its goal of producing 10 million metric tons of sugar cane. The occasion was a welcome-home speech for a handful of Cuban fishermen who had been released after being captured by an anti-Castro exile group. Castro said the news that the sugar harvest yield was less than planned was "hard to take." On July 24, the harvest officially ended with 8.5 tons of production. It was a record amount, but not the 10 million tons that Castro had vowed the country would produce and which, he said, could be used as a measuring stick to judge the Cuban Revolution.

Two days later, Castro offered briefly to resign. He took his share of the blame for the failure to meet the sugar goal he had promised. "I do not pretend to indicate that I think some responsibilities do not belong to me and the entire leadership of the Revolution," Castro told thousands massed in Havana's Plaza de la Revolucion to mark the tenth anniversary of his rule. "Regrettably this self-criticism cannot be easily accompanied by other solutions." But then he suggested one. "It would be better to say to the people: 'Seek someone else, look for others.' In truth, for my part, it would be better, but it would be hypocritical." Because, he explained, "our problems cannot be resolved by replacing the revolution's leaders, which our people can do when they want to at the time they want to, and right now if they want to." And, of course, as Castro knew before he spoke, the people didn't want to and couldn't replace him.

For my part, I was sorry the big effort for the 10 million tons had failed, but I also felt exonerated in reporting that the Cuban sugar harvest would probably fail to make its goal.

Chapter Nine

SOVIET FRIENDSHIP

When Castro publicly criticized the Soviet Union in early 1968 for refusing to increase its crude oil exports to Cuba, I was sought out almost immediately by Mikhail Roy, a correspondent for the Soviet news agency Novosti. Mikhail was my best contact among the many East Bloc journalists.

Mikhail presented me with figures showing the Soviet Union had never reduced its oil deliveries to Cuba. That, of course, was not Castro's point. The Cuban leader was objecting to the fact that the Soviet Union had refused Cuba's request for an 8 percent increase in crude oil. But Mikhail's counterpoint that Moscow's oil exports to Cuba had not been cut was the way the Soviet Union wanted it to be seen by the West. Mikhail was, after all, just doing part of his job — spreading disinformation — only this time it was about a partner, not a Cold War target. I had little doubt then and even less within a month that Mikhail had been a pupil, perhaps a graduate of one of Moscow's many cadres, most likely the KGB.

Cuba's little fuss with the Soviet Union over oil was not all that surprising. Castro had picked on Moscow before for

Soviet trade with Latin American countries that opposed the Havana regime and over Castro's armed revolution adventures. Cubans and Soviets didn't seem to socialize easily. I never saw a Soviet man fraternizing with any of Cuba's Afro-Cuban women. It made me wonder at times if the Soviets would have been in Cuba at all had Castro also been black.

Mikhail had befriended me soon after I arrived in Havana. I suppose he was assigned to me. Novosti had a reputation for spying, including counter-intelligence. After Castro's OLAS speech that criticized me, Mikhail and his bosses may have deduced I was his U.S. counterpart. Some but not all of his reports about me may eventually have found their way to Cuban intelligence. All Soviet intelligence matters, a friend at the British Embassy insisted, were supposed to. Whatever the reckoning, it was obviously good for him to have contact with the only American journalist in Cuba. I was glad to have a Soviet source, of sorts. We were both on our first overseas assignment, and we became professional semi-friends.

One day he surprised Ann and me with a visit to the AP apartment, where he proudly presented her with a tiny plastic model of the Soviet Union's Sputnik, the first space satellite. The 1957 Soviet achievement, which occurred while Castro was fighting the Batista dictatorship in the Sierra Maestra, had worried the United States, particularly the military, a thousand times more than sporadic reports of guerrilla warfare 90 miles from Florida. Sputnik, however, had spurred the American scientific community to more than catch up by 1968. In fact, by then, the United States was only a year away from landing on the moon.

Mikhail showed a genuine interest in almost all things American and seemed especially curious that my wife had accompanied me to Cuba. He had, he explained, left his wife in Moscow because of his job. He didn't ask the question, but it was clear he wondered why I hadn't. I told him Ann wasn't completely out of her element. She had studied in Mexico and was fluent in Spanish. She had been a journalist on the Texas paper where we both worked and had accompanied me to Chile on a scholarship from the Inter-American Press Association. In its annual reports, the U.S.-dominated conservative organization regularly put Cuba in the same class as Haiti and North Korea, accusing Castro of violating press freedom and human rights. The organization had little to do directly with its scholars, but the scholarship was a piece of my background the Cuban screeners must have missed in permitting my entry.

One morning I went to Mikhail's apartment at his request ostensibly to discuss a Soviet propaganda film playing in Havana. Instead, we discussed the Cuban economy over cognac and chocolates, a combination I do not recommend at that time of day. At 10:45 he said he must be excused to see the Soviet ambassador at 11 a.m. He said he visited the Soviet embassy daily at that hour. It was part of his job reporting to the embassy daily.

Three weeks after the announcement of gasoline rationing, the Central Committee of the Cuban Communist Party went into a marathon secret session in Havana. There were a half dozen rumors about the reason why, but the most prevalent was that "old" Soviet-line members of the party were in trouble. Western diplomatic sources were in the dark. Paco Teira said he had heard that rumor but had no confirmation. I had never used him as a lone source and had no intention of doing so now. Finally, I reached Mikhail. He agreed at once to meet me but asked that it be in a public place.

I met him at the Hotel Nacional at mid-afternoon. We opted for the cocktail lounge to avoid the heavy pedestrian traffic in the lobby. Except for the bartender, the lounge was empty, so we took a table. The bartender was just out of hearing distance. We spoke our common language, Spanish. There was no attempt on the part of either of us to be furtive. Besides, in those days in Cuba, or elsewhere, who could possibly conclude that a Soviet and an American were collaborating on anything of importance?

I asked Mikhail what had kept the Central Committee in session so long. After explaining that the Soviet Union was still Cuba's most loyal and generous brother, Mikhail began by acknowledging Moscow and Havana had some basic policy differences. It was a new level of candor for him. Those differences, he said with little detail, had resulted in 35 to 40 Cuban party members being examined by the Central Committee and that this group might be removed from the party for "political reasons." He mentioned no names, but he identified the party members being examined as longtime Cuban communists. He said they all respected Castro but disagreed with his economic policies and his campaign to export revolution to Latin America. In other words, they espoused the Soviet line.

That was enough for a story, and I wrote it. The next day, the newspaper *Granma*, the official voice of the Cuban Communist Party announced that 37 party members headed by old-time communist Anibal Escalante, whom Castro had purged from the party for "sectarianism" six years earlier, would be tried for conspiring against the government. No charges were specified. The group was denounced as a "microfaction" within the party. And Mikhail Roy's name was in the paper. The paper said he had been followed by the DSE, the secret police, and had been seen clandestinely meeting one of the conspiracy's leaders. He and a handful of other unmentioned Soviets were expelled, and I never saw him again. But I was thankful our meeting had been in a public place, remembering it was at his request. In my many years in journalism, I have never had a source that was closer to the story.

The best news source in Cuba, of course, was Fidel Castro. Still is. His speeches were his versions of news conferences. That's as close as he came to meeting the press in my time.

Few Cuban journalists had access to Castro, or to his inner circle. If Castro didn't say something of import in one of his speeches or in one of his infrequent interviews (and those almost always were given only to big name media, people, or political figures), news simply had to trickle down through the system.

The government had news conferences now and then for cultural events to announce agricultural projects or report on them and to introduce visiting guests of the Revolution. The guests usually denounced the United States for imperialism and its military intervention in Vietnam. Black American visitors added racial oppression to the attacks on the U.S. system. I covered most of these news conferences. Irving Davis, who was introduced as a joint director of foreign relations for the Student Nonviolent Coordinating Committee, typified those Americans. He told his news conference attendees that "30 million Afro-Americans still were political prisoners" but he was in Havana "to tell the world we will get our freedom." There were lots of statements like that in the United States in the 1960s, and I suspected as I sent the story to the AP in New York that it would get more notice in Havana than it would in the United States.

My available records show I wrote to Castro three times asking for interviews. I also wrote once to his longtime friend and confidante, the late Celia Sanchez, asking for her help. Despite always chilly receptions, I also kept making verbal requests regularly at the Foreign Affairs Ministry. I knew at one time in his revolutionary days Castro had considered news of Cuba going abroad important for the Revolution and had used such news as a propaganda tool. He did this to help raise funds in the United States for his guerrilla war against the Batista's dictatorship.

But after the United States broke relations with Cuba, tried to invade it, and forced the Soviet Union to withdraw the missiles that Castro wanted kept on the island, his tune changed. I had heard him more than once deplore news reports by the Western news agencies, especially AP and UPI. Through the years he has received and been interviewed by U.S. television news personalities, journalists on special assignments, people writing books (not all of them pro-Castro), American congressmen, politicians, industrialists, and entertainment celebrities. Who he hasn't abided are people who, as he said when he criticized me, "write daily" from Cuba. In other words, resident foreign correspondents above all Americans.

Unsurprisingly and understandable for his purposes, Castro has been selective about who he was willing to talk to. But sometimes his choices have seemed ridiculous. I witnessed one such choice at the end of 1968, when Castro invited Kristi Witker, representing *Vogue* magazine to the annual celebration scheduled on January 2, 1969, to mark 10 years of Cuban Revolution. An ex-model, Witker seemed uninformed about both Castro and the Revolution when I talked to her in my office. Nonetheless, Castro invited her to the presidential palace. As it turned out, their meeting was brief and not illuminating from a news standpoint. She later said she became better acquainted with the late Rene Vallejo, Castro's physician, than with the Cuban leader during her brief stay in Havana and backed up that information by later supplying me with a medicine that quickly cured a skin disease that had me typing with gloves on. Apparently the affliction was widely known in Cuba.

My other affliction, a lack of good permanent news sources, was more persistent. I had none I could trust. Still, Castro's speeches were one of the best sources available, and I spent many long hours going over the newspaper text of his two and three-hour orations. His delivery, usually without a written text, was stunning, emotional, and instructive. He often announced plans for the future and explained Cuba's policies. With what seemed like increasing regularity in 1967 and much of 1968, he criticized the Soviet Union. He reported, sometimes in detail, the faults and mistakes of the Revolution and almost always urged Cubans to work harder and guard against Yankee imperialism. After *Playa Giron* (the Bay of Pigs), he began closing his speeches with the slogan, "Fatherland or death we will win." He has never abandoned the slogan.

The official Cuban Communist Party newspaper, *Granma*, also was a good source. Even better sometimes were the provincial newspapers and they often had a more homey quality. Cuban radio stations, Havana television and the Cuban news agency were helpful but heavy on propaganda. I remember one old American "Our Gang" (later renamed "the Little Rascals") film clip shown on Havana television that was a propaganda jewel. The episode showed the child actors building a car to enter in America's Soap Box Derby. At the conclusion, the Havana TV announcer said the film showed how Detroit was deceiving American youth into a life of capitalist slavery to work for Ford and General Motors. Cuban television also made regular fun of Superman and his vow to fight for "truth justice and the American way," which it depicted as decadent, dehumanizing and violent.

If you wanted an official quote, you had to try to dig one out of somebody. And if you got an anti-Castro quote invariably you were asked by the person who spoke not to use his or her name. As a rule a correspondent could talk to anybody who would talk to him.

In writing stories about Cuba or Castro, I became increasingly aware of using the word "however." It seemed necessary to use it often to explain that some things happening in Cuba were neither all black nor all white, or that there often were exceptions to a policy or a rule. Mexico was an example. It was the only Latin American country that had diplomatic relations with Havana, and because it did Castro's government overlooked the rampant corruption that pervaded Mexico's super capitalistic economy and the government's neglect of its poor.

When I thought of the word "however," I often was reminded of the title of one of the first books about Cuba I read before going to Havana, *Cuba Island of Paradox*, by Ruby Hart Phillips. She had been a *New York Times* correspondent before and for a while after Castro came to power and had seen a lot of "howevers" in her time. Castro's Revolution had multiplied the paradoxes since then.

Officially the Ministerio de Relaciones Exteriores (MINREX the acronym in Spanish for Foreign Affairs Ministry) was supposed to be the source of information for foreign correspondents. It was worse than useless and often a barrier. If a question to MINREX was considered "provocative," you could lose the chance to contact an official source. Sometimes my reputation and AP's preceded me. A Transportation Ministry official once told me "we don't give news to imperialist agencies." If this sounds like Castro had a hand in almost everything in those days it is only a slight exaggeration. He couldn't and didn't manage everything. But he eventually learned about most everything of importance and definitely was in control. Almost all of Cuba's agricultural experiments were initiated by Castro. He decided foreign policy and of course was the country's leading Marxist, the creator of Cuban revolutionary communism and the commander-in-chief of the armed forces. In Cuba he remained simply Fidel. So I thought of him like that but in news stories he was always Castro.

The Cold War in the late 1960s was very visible in Cuba as evidenced by the number of embassies represented in Havana. On one side there was the Soviet bloc plus Vietnam, North Korea and China. None of those was direct sources for me. But there were always the Western embassies: the British, the Dutch, the Canadians, the Belgians, the Israelis, and sometimes the French. All the Westerners were useful on Cuba's economic affairs. But they often asked more questions than they answered. Their diplomatic receptions, however, had to be checked out because sometimes there was useful background information, and now and then Castro would show up at one of them. However, the few times he did I never got into the room where he was before he was gone.

From time to time I still looked over my shoulder and saw nothing. But I had noted two obvious and clumsy attempts to entrap me. Both had been telephone calls to the AP office from women speaking in accented English and asking if I wanted to make love. I had hung up on both of them. Those made me wonder if entrapment had been part of Mikhail's Roy's assignment. I liked to think it wasn't.

Chapter Ten

POLITICS, ALWAYS POLITICS

One morning after waking up I sipped coffee on my terrace and waved to that pleasant old communist Rene Portocarrero on the balcony below and said to myself, "You are not a spy, don't write like one." Don't file stories that might make you look even faintly like a Kim Philby, Britain's infamous double agent who reported for the *Times of London* before he finally defected to Moscow. Stay away, for awhile, I told myself, from stories with a political bent.

But I couldn't resist one more. At the end of March, as Cuba began struggling with Castro's nationalization, President Lyndon Johnson announced he would not seek reelection. Johnson and his family had been brutal propaganda targets on Cuban television. One TV spot showed a Johnson daughter giving birth to a pig. The U.S. president was particularly despised because American military involvement in Vietnam had escalated during his administration. But officials at the Foreign Ministry said the news that Johnson would not run again wasn't too important — that whoever was in the White House, the U.S.

policy on Cuba would remain anti-Castro, anti-Cuban, anti-Revolution. I wrote a reaction story to that effect.

I also wrote a story for the AP house organ on how I tried to cover the country. I described Cubans as "generally a friendly lot ready to talk even to a *Yanqui* newsman based in Cuba." Over the years my assessment of Cubans as friendly people proved to be an understatement. Since then, I have been shot at in Portugal, hit by a police baton in Madrid, faced Uzis in Ecuador and FLN automatic weapons several times in Peru, but nobody ever pointed a gun at me in Cuba. I saw more automatic weapons on the streets of Franco's Spain than I ever saw in Cuba. The Revolution's soldiers I encountered in Havana and elsewhere in Cuba kept their handguns holstered. They turned me away with finger *wagglesa* gesture I quickly learned to respect. Most of them probably had no idea I was an American. Of course, Cuban intelligence did. I knew that the unit of the Committees for the Defense of the Revolution in my apartment building kept track of my comings and goings. I was certain that both the apartment and office telephones were tapped. But I had seen no sign of anyone following me.

About this time the official Cuban Communist Party newspaper *Granma* ran a story of mine on its front page about how medical and health care in Cuba had improved under Castro. The motive, undoubtedly, was to show that even the AP recognized the Revolution had made gains for the good of the country. I felt somewhat pardoned. Then Radio Rebelde called the office and wanted to begin taking the AP news wire in Spanish from New York. I had no idea how much to charge the radio station in Cuban pesos (the money was useless for the AP outside of Cuba and there was no way to get it out anyway), but I gave them a figure. The station quickly agreed, and, like all the AP clients in Cuba, never missed a payment. My level of paranoia plunged. I concentrated more than ever on nonpolitical reporting.

I did a story on a new sugar-cane combine developed by Cuban engineers — a machine supposedly able to outperform heavier and clumsier Soviet reapers. The Cuban machine, modified from the Soviet combine, was named the "Liberator" by Castro because he said "it will liberate man from the rough work of cutting cane." Castro could have mentioned women among those to be liberated from the machete because, along with thousands of men, they, too, were being mobilized to meet Castro's announced goal of a record 10 million tons of sugar production in 1970.

Castro also began a program to build an agricultural "Green Belt" around Havana to increase the nation's food supply. Thousands singing revolutionary songs at the urging of the Committees for the Defense of the Revolution (CDR) rode in trucks to the countryside to plant crops. Those who didn't volunteer were considered by CDR leaders to be anti-patriotic and on the edge of being counterrevolutionary. Many displaced by nationalization spent their weekends riding to the outskirts of Havana to set out coffee plants from the mountains of Mexico — at nearly sea level. The idea seemed novel and risky. A bean plant from India called gandul was tried. It turned out to be too tough to harvest successfully. The Green Belt turned brown, one of several government agricultural experiments that failed. But the mobilizations kept people focused as the effects of nationalization worsened. Was this political news that I was reporting?

During a Castro speech, a grizzled old peasant on the front row of the outdoor audience noted a long Trinidad cigar (one of Castro's favorites for a time) peeking out of the prime minister's olive green shirt. "Comandante," he asked "how come you have a cigar and I don't?" Castro gave him the cigar and began a 10-minute explanation of why the hard times were necessary.

With all the bars closed, the only place to get an alcoholic drink was in a restaurant. But to obtain a cocktail, the customer had to eat. Too often there was neither food nor drink. Among the bars closed was Sloppy Joe's, a Havana meeting place for tourists and visiting American movie stars in pre-Castro days. It had been kept intact by the National Institute of the Tourist Industry with photographs of former American movie favorites like Tyrone Power and Linda Darnell. Still open, but short of rum (most of it was being exported to earn hard currency), it was the Floridita American writer Ernest Hemingway's favorite. It was a bar-restaurant with a limited menu.

On the Ramblas in Old Havana was the British Club, formerly the American Club, where members and invited guests, usually all foreigners, ate steak and kidney pie once a week in the former American All States Room. Only 48 states were represented on the walls of the club room. Alaska and Hawaii became states after Castro came to power. The club also showed movies. One of the favorites was "Our Man in Havana." A couple of retired sugar engineers could usually be found in the club's reading room, leafing through copies of month-old British newspapers. The retirees were valuable sources for technical information on how the Revolution was doing with sugar production.

There was also one operating golf course in Cuba, the British Rovers Club on Havana's outskirts. It abutted a military installation whose presence prohibited looking for lost balls, which were as treasured in those hard times as black beans and rice. Diplomats said the sound of small arms fire often interrupted their putting. A few old caddies helped players around the scrubby 9-hole course. Castro promoted baseball, track, boxing, and basketball, but not golf. He and Che Guevara reportedly had tried it one time and given up in disgust. Besides, it was a capitalist's game.

Faced with long lines at restaurants and struggling with food rationing, Cubans turned, along with Castro, to Havana's ultra modern ice cream parlor, the Coppelia. It became the most popular place in downtown Havana, with lines that spread out like a spider's web. Thirty years later, Coppelia has more flavors and is still popular. It was the setting for an exported 1990s Cuban movie, "Strawberry and Chocolate," which touched on anti-revolutionary feelings and homosexuality, subjects that existed but were not publicly allowed in 1968.

Lesbianism was not mentioned or addressed at all in the 1960s. Heterosexuality, however, was. The government established and managed several motel-hotels called *posadas*, where lovers could spend an hour or two. The cost was minimal, and there were often long queues of anxious couples waiting to get in. Castro recognized the problem, and the government then suggested impatient youths should use the privacy of some of Havana's bosques — wooded parks — instead of paying and waiting in line. The tropical climate, rough ground, and insects bollixed the idea.

I found it harder to write good news about Cuba, although I tried. I did a story on free weddings at the Wedding Palace in downtown Havana, by far the most plush of free marriage sites in four of the country's six provinces. The elegant building on the Prado in Old Havana boasted marble stairways, gold leaf in the ceiling, chandeliers, velvet furniture, and ornate mirrors. In pre-Castro days it was the Spanish Casinoa millionaire's gambling playground. It was now run by the Ministry of Justice. About 50 couples a day wed there. The free part included the ceremony and the use of the palace. But couples had to pay for drinks, food, photographs, and, if they were so inclined, a big old black Cadillac to drive them away. No rice was thrown. It was rationed.

Divorce, in effect, was also free. Partners could free themselves of their companions simply by declaring to authorities he or she wanted to end the marriage. There was no property to divide, no lawyers' fees. Child custody could be handled by the state-run nursery-kindergarten schools. The Foreign Ministry press section declined to give information on abortions, except to say that they were legal. The ministry repeatedly responded to questions about birth control by saying it was unneeded because the Revolution, meaning the government, would and could provide for any increase in population.

After Castro announced that there would be no Christmas holidays because there was too much work to be done, I decided to see how religion was doing under so-called Godless communism. I found Catholicism alive but not very well in Catholic Cuba. Although church attendance was never outstanding before, Castro did not attract any more worshippers during the country's hard times. Most worshippers were older people. The young, even had they been interested, were busy working in agriculture. There was still a papal nuncio in Cuba. The Vatican had never broken diplomatic relations. Vatican sources told me that only about 2 percent of the population could have been considered regular church goers before Castro came to power in 1959.

Until 1961, there were 750 priests and 3,000 nuns. Seven years later about 200 nuns and 220 priests — 100 of them Cubans — remained. One of them was Carlos Manuel de Cespedes, great grandson of a Cuban hero who launched the first insurrection against Spain in 1868. Father Cespedes was rector of a two-centuries old seminary in Havana. He recalled that before communism became official in 1961, some priests spoke against it. "You are still free to do it if you want," he said. "But nobody will. It's useless." He obviously feared no retribution from the government and was one of the few sources who allowed his name to be used. Being a great grandson of a Cuban hero admired by Castro undoubtedly gave him a special status. But Castro, Jesuit-educated in his early years, had left the church, largely alone, despite expelling scores of priests and closing more than 100 Catholic schools in the early days of the Revolution. There was, in fact, no reason for the communist government to worry about the Catholic church. It had never been a decisive political force in the past.

Relations between Castro's communist government and the Vatican were strained and seldom mentioned, but they did continue. Monsignor Cesar Zacchi was the current *charge d'affaires ad interim* of the Holy See in Cuba. His name seldom appeared in the newspapers. Bishops and other members of the church hierarchy were allowed to travel in and out of Cuba without hindrance and did, for example, in 1968, when they went to a church conference in Colombia.

Before you could say *Yanqui imperialismo*, I found myself back on the political news trail. I did a story saying Castro's popularity appeared to be at one of the lowest points since he had come to power. Discontented Cubans were complaining mostly about living conditions, increasing government pressure to demand more while giving less. Crude wall drawings declared "Down With Fidel, down with communism." There was suspected sabotage at some government plants in rural areas. Some Havana high school students were censured for distributing anti-government literature. During an assembly honoring Vietnam's Ho Chi Minh at Havana University, a handful of students shouted "down with Vietnam, we're hungry." A publication of the Communist Party Central Committee explained: "We are going through a hard period difficult in the life of our Revolution."

Young people seemed the most disaffected with the government. In one of the nearly 400 People's Courts, Court No. 6 of Vedado, I attended the trial of two teenage boys who had bought a Beatles record on the black market for 25 pesos (officially $25). "Why don't you want to be like Che?" one of the judges asked.

Most of the unrest, if it could be called that, was consumer-oriented. And it was nothing like the early 1960s, when anti-Castroites armed and organized an unsuccessful revolt in the Sierra Maestra. Despite problems, Cubans still seemed ahead of most of the common folks in Mexico and South America. Cuban peasants and workers had free health care, education, and social services, minus the rampant corruption that pervaded governments in Latin America.

Then Castro welcomed a surprise visitor to Havana, a Yankee who had been one of the many American investors in Cuba before communism. The Cuban prime minister frequently received selected Western visitors without much fanfare. Such was the case of industrialist Cyrus Eaton of Cleveland, Ohio. Obviously, Castro had been briefed on Eaton's political feelings about the new Cuba before Eaton arrived in Havana in December of 1968. But the industrialist and the Cuban leader, more than 40 years the American's junior, apparently hit it off from the start. Castro showed his liking for the chairman of the board of the Chesapeake and Ohio Railway Company by presenting Eaton with a cake on Eaton's 85th birthday. He also went to a party for Eaton, attended by both the Soviet (representing the East) and Swiss (representing the West) ambassadors.

Eaton spent 10 days in Cuba and was taken on a tour of agricultural projects by Castro. Before Eaton left, he asked me to breakfast and told me that a paint company he owned before Castro came to power had been taken over by the

Cuban government and he had no interest in getting it back. In fact, he said he was happy the Havana government had it. His position ran counter to demands by most U.S. corporations, seeking compensation for property seized in the early 1960s by the Castro government. Years later, the compensation fuss still simmers in Washington, but not in Havana.

As Castro moved nearer to his 10th anniversary in power, I wrote a story saying there was less than a slim chance, despite the hard times, of him being overthrown. Earlier, the *San Diego Union* had run another story of mine about Castro saying that after nine years of aiming, he was trying to close in on making Cuba the first truly communist country in the world. The headline, which I presumed and hoped Castro never saw asked: "How Far Can Castro Turn the Screws?" I could have answered that. Quite a bit, in fact. He still had wide support from Cubans as they struggled through their toughest economic year. His new challenges were to be caused principally by events abroad.

Chapter Eleven

CASTROESE

"**S**ome of the things we are going to state here will be in some cases in contradiction with the emotions of many," Castro told the nation in a speech from a television studio two days after the Soviet invasion of Czechoslovakia on August 21, 1968. It was one of his rare understatements. Nobody had taken a poll, but it would not have been a stretch of the imagination to think that the majority of Cubans could not believe their ears when Castro said the Cuban government stood behind the Soviet move, even as the Red Army tanks began patrolling the streets of Prague.

For years Castro had been preaching to Cubans that independence meant sovereignty for Cuba, and sovereignty was a sacred principle. And now the Soviets had trampled all over that tenet, and the Revolution's leader was suddenly supporting such action.

Before Castro spoke there were signs Cubans did not back the Soviet Union's action. The communist youth newspaper *Juventud Rebelde* in a front-page headline, recklessly branded the Soviet action an "invasion." The mood on Havana's streets from the few people who would talk to me about it was clearly anti-Soviet. Some said they didn't understand the Soviet action. Most were waiting for Castro to lash out at the Soviets for violating Czechoslovakia's sovereignty.

The Czech embassy in Havana denied the Prague government had agreed in any manner to the "occupation" of its land. A group of Czech sailors and technicians staged a street protest in Havana with posters saying "Russians Go Home."

Castro did not avoid the sovereignty issue. But before he faced it, he also warned his audience that, besides contradicting "the emotions of many Cubans," the government's analysis (*his* analysis) could also contradict "our own interests ... and constitute serious risks for our country."

In speaking of Cuba's analysis of the Soviet action in Czechoslovakia, Castro used the words "we" and "our" repeatedly, when in reality he meant the government and the Cuban Communist Party leadership, not the people.

"We," he said, "became suspicious of the 'liberalization' in Czechoslovakia when it began to receive the praise, support, or enthusiastic applause of the imperialist press."

After studying the liberalization, Castro said "we considered that Czechoslovakia was moving toward a counterrevolutionary situation toward capitalism and into the arms of imperialism. (Elsewhere in the speech he mentioned pro-Yankee spies.)

"So," he continued "this defines our first position in relation to the specific fact of the action taken by a group of socialist countries. That is, we consider that it was absolutely necessary at all costs, in one way or another, to prevent this eventuality from taking place."

As for Czech sovereignty, Castro's words seemed reminiscent of the days when he was a young lawyer-rebel and had found an explanation for why his armed attack on the Moncada army barracks fifteen years earlier was legal . He declared: "What cannot be denied here is that the sovereignty of the Czechoslovak state was violated ... I am going to refer ... to our concept of sovereignty to legal principles and political principles. From a legal point of view, this (the Soviet invasion) cannot be justified. This is very clear. In our opinion, the decision made concerning Czechoslovakia can only be explained from a political point of view, not from a legal point of view. Not the slightest trace of legality exists. Frankly, none whatever."

So there it was ,stated simply in Castroese. The Soviet military action in Czechoslovakia was not legal, but that did not matter. It was necessary politically. The Cuban nation now had been so informed. It was now my task to storify that explanation for the rest of the world. In many world capitals leaders would not be surprised that Castro had backed the Soviet invasion. Of course he would. Wasn't Cuba 90 per cent dependent on Soviet financing?

Castro showed he recognized that. When he got to "the risks" Cuba was making by showing support for the Soviet invasion, he indicated Cuba expected something from Moscow in return. "We ask ourselves: Will Warsaw Pact divisions also be sent to Vietnam if the Yankee imperialists step up their aggression against that country and the people of Vietnam request that aid? Will they send the divisions of the Warsaw Pact to the Democratic People's Republic of (North)) Korea if the Yankee imperialists attack that country?" And lastly: "Will they send divisions of the Warsaw Pact to Cuba if the Yankee imperialists attack our country or even in the case of the threat of a Yankee imperialist attack on our country if our country requests it?"

The Soviet Union, Castro knew, had already answered his questions about sending troops to defend Cuba from the United States obliquely replied to in 1961 when Moscow had made no such move against the U.S.-backed Bay of Pigs attack and directly answered in 1962 when the Kremlin withdrew its missiles from Cuba over Castro's protests. If not Soviet bloc troops, then what could Castro settle for in backing what he said was clearly a violation of sovereignty in Moscow's invasion of Czechoslovakia?

More oil was the answer, and substantial economic and technical aid, primarily financial support that, unknown to either Moscow or Havana at the time, was destined to help keep Cuba afloat until the Soviet Union died in 1991. It was clear that Castro needed money, but ,as he frankly explained to the Cuban nation, that was not the primary motive he had in endorsing the Soviet invasion of Czechoslovakia. He had, as he said, simply opted for a political principle as old as war itself: If a country's politics are threatening to your country, invasion of that country is acceptable, and in Czechoslovakia's case that was absolutely necessary.

In backing the Soviet invasion, however, Castro had been forced into the capitalistic-like position of putting his mouth where the money was, and this less than a month after he told his July 26 audience that Cuba's goal was to eventually have true communism, where money would no longer be needed. Beyond noting that the Soviet Union was Cuba's major financial supporter and primary trading partner, I did not include the above observations in my story. I wrote instead with the premise that Castro's words would speak for themselves. Such political expediency, nonetheless, was obviously a surprise for many in Cuba. But it was also very much in character with Castro's past. He had used it in his student days in organizing and raising funds for the guerrilla movement in his first days in power. He also could draw the line at too much compromise and said so near the end of his speech. Cuba, he said had no interest in bettering relations with the United States as long as it was "the international gendarme bulwark of world reaction" and an "aggressor in Vietnam, an aggressor in the Dominican Republic, and an intervener in revolutionary movements." He declared: "Never, even under any circumstance, even the most difficult circumstance, will this country approach the imperialist government of the United States—not even should it one day place us in the situation of having to choose between continued existence of the Revolution or such a step ... that would be the moment at which the Revolution would have ceased to exist." He added that Cubans would prefer to "disappear with the Revolution rather than survive at such a price."

Castro also threw ice water on any real chance of future relations with the United States. "We are not interested in economic relations and we are even less interested in diplomatic relations of any kind," he told his compatriots.

It was tough talk for eight million people living only ninety miles from a powerful enemy that already had gone half way around the world to fight what it perceived as a dire communist threat in Asia. Would Castro stand by all those declarations today or, for the life of the Revolution, would he modify them? It was not a question that occurred to me at the end of that summer.

After Castro's stance supporting Moscow in the Czech invasion increased, Soviet aid was neither immediate nor visible. But backing at home for Castro's position was. The government-organized Committees for the Defense of the Revolution (CDR) took to the streets, declaring solidarity with the prime minister. Cuba's controlled media joined in. Vilma Espin, wife of Castro's younger brother Raul and head of the Federation of Cuban Women, said every member of her organization should be proud to have confidence in the nation's leader.

On September 28, the founding date of the CDR, Castro made his annual speech, praising its two million members and urging everybody in the country to work harder and longer. He asked Cubans to concentrate on producing a record 10 million tons of sugar in 1970. Perhaps by then the first rewards for Cuba's support in the squelching of the Prague Spring would start showing up, along with money from the hoped-for record sugar harvest. If not, Cuba's leader surely could explain the reason for failure in Castroese, but I wouldn't be there to report it.

Chapter Twelve

FIDEL, FACE TO FACE

If 1968 was a difficult year for Cuba, it was also a tough time for the United States. The Tet offensive in Vietnam at the end of January signaled to Americans they were losing a war that many never understood in the first place. U.S. setbacks in Vietnam combined with anti-war protests at home finally wore down President Lyndon Johnson. He announced that he would not seek reelection. Within a week of Johnson's decision, the Reverend Martin Luther King, the country's civil rights leader, was assassinated. Two months later, Sen. Robert Kennedy, a candidate for president, died from an assassin's bullet. Cubans heard and read daily about all the problems of their government's despised colossus to the north.

Then somebody at the Foreign Ministry press section — it may have been Oscar Lujones, unless he had already been swallowed up by the bureaucracy or fallen into disfavor by that summer — invited me to cover a speech by Castro on the south coast. I jumped at the chance, because I wanted to see Castro in action in the countryside and get a feel of the nationalization's effect there. I was transported to the scene in a Foreign Ministry car, an old black American sedan, an Oldsmobile. People lining the road from Havana to the speech site cheered and waved at me as part of the official party. I waved back, but I didn't get a chance to talk to any of them.

At the town of Batabano loudspeakers around the platform where Castro was to speak blared out "The 26th of July March," the nation's post-Castro hymn. The words at the start *"Adelante todos Cubanos"* (Forward all Cubans) were stirring. So was the crowd's reaction. Those who knew the words sang; the rest clapped and shouted. When Castro arrived, as usual by an unannounced route for security reasons, everybody seemed to sense his presence before they saw him. They started cheering.

Midway through Castro's speech a downpour began — not an unusual happening at Castro's outdoor speeches. But it was my first experience at watching the Cuban leader do what he was reported to have done many times during his guerrilla life in the Sierra Maestra — accommodate nature. In fact, nature seemed to be on his side. Lightning and thunder served to emphasize his words and gestures. His olive green uniform turned dark with rain and his beard glistened with raindrops as he drew repeated cheers from the crowd. It's often very hot in Cuba in July, and nobody, least of all the speaker, minded the rain.

Castro's appearance at Batabano was a big event for that area. Like many of his outdoor speeches, it was a social occasion as well, even more so in that hard summer of 1968. Nobody left. I know, because I was standing on the front row, looking at the gun barrels of soldiers who held back people crowded around the front of the elevated platform, where the Cuban leader stood. From there I could also look back at the mass of wet, upturned faces. The scene took on a religious air. Castro sounded like an evangelist; his words like a sermon. I don't remember much of anything he said, and it wouldn't have helped if I had. The rain had turned my notebook to mush. But I wasn't concerned. I knew Stanley Graham back in Havana would have most of the important parts written down when I got back to the office.

As Castro left the platform at the end of his speech, he came my way. I told a ministry official I had a question for Castro. The official yelled at Castro that the AP man was nearby. Castro stopped and waited for me to speak. I knew what I wanted to ask: His opinion about the recent assassinations in the United States of Sen. Kennedy and the Rev. King. I wanted to go with the Kennedy question first. To this day I have no idea exactly why.

But outside of perhaps a handful of Americans in the right places in Washington, I did not know as I got ready to put my question to Castro that Robert Kennedy in 1962 had headed the U.S. government's "Operation Mongoose," a top-secret program aimed, according to Senate Intelligence Committee reports made public in 1975, at "getting rid" of Castro. I doubt if the Cuban leader knew then about the plot either as he faced me in the rain.

So I asked him about Kennedy's slaying first. If Castro was surprised by the question, he didn't show it. Instead he seemed interested. Looking me straight in the eye he replied he was saddened by the act. He then started to say something about deploring assassinations, but the conversation was abruptly interrupted as the crowd surged around us and security forced me to move on. Thus ended my first and only face-to-face meeting with Fidel Castro.

The next day I wrote a letter, addressing it not to the prime minister, but to Comandante Dr. Fidel Castro, hoping those more familiar titles and our brief encounter would improve the chances of an interview. Wes Gallagher, the president and general manager of the Associated Press, was due to arrive the next day for a week's stay in Cuba, noting that as head of the AP, he was the person most responsible for seeing to it that the news agency "maintained the standard of objectivity." But my letter to Castro, like all the rest I had written, was never answered.

Gallagher had been trying for some time to come to Cuba, the first head of the AP to do so since Castro had taken power. Gallagher liked to visit his reporters in the field. A former World War II war correspondent, he already had been to Vietnam, where he had sent some of the AP's best, and they had rewarded his judgment by bringing back Pulitzer Prizes in both news and photos. As head of the world's largest news gathering organization, Gallagher was tough, demanding and fair. Although his penchant for wanting to see his reporters on the job also applied in the United States, it was the people working overseas he enjoyed visiting the most. He had the journalist's curiosity. But after I got to know him just a bit, I suspected he also was catering to his nostalgia that, for a few hours, he would prefer to be reporting again, not just running things as the AP's chief executive from his seventh floor office at 50 Rockefeller Plaza. Whatever his feelings, they had, over the years, enforced his belief that foreign correspondents, at least the good ones, usually knew more about what they were reporting on than the editors working on their copy back home. If not, they didn't last long in Cairo, Saigon, or Moscow.

So I hadn't been totally surprised when he began pushing buttons to try to visit Cuba. I had a faint recollection that he had mentioned something to that effect when he called me to his office a year earlier to tell me I was going to Havana. He apparently felt the time was ripe to try for such a visit.

In response to his request, I had gone to the Foreign Ministry to ask if Gallagher could come to Cuba to see the Cuban Revolution and inspect the AP bureau, which hadn't been looked at by anybody with authority since before Castro. The ministry told me he should apply through the Czech embassy in Washington, the channel for Cuban matters in the United States. The fact that I didn't get an outright "no" was encouraging. That, and a couple of other signals allowed me to feel that perhaps I was becoming officially less of an enemy. A few weeks later I was informed that Gallagher had been approved, along with several other American journalists, to attend the annual July 26 celebration, marking the anniversary of Castro's attack on the Moncada army barracks in 1953. The date had been honored each year since Castro's forces took over Cuba. It marked Castro's first armed attack against the Batista dictatorship. The assault failed, and Castro went to prison for almost two years, but the attack openly confirmed his argument that armed revolt was the only way to free Cuba from a corrupt, mismanaged dictatorship and from the yoke of the United States.

When the government told me that Gallagher could come to Cuba, I asked again for an interview with Castro, suggesting it could be an opportunity for Castro to get a worldwide audience via AP. Gallagher had not mentioned anything about an interview. But I thought his presence in Cuba would present a news opportunity for the AP that should not be ignored, despite the odds against Castro granting an interview. The government responded quickly: no interview, no explanation.

The AP boss arrived in Havana disgusted with Mexican officialdom that had delayed his departure from Mexico for Cuba. It was a feeling I came to share sometime later when the Mexican Embassy in Havana delayed giving me the paperwork to pass through Mexico. The embassy officer in Havana was waiting for a bribe he never got. Cubans going that route told me the standard price was $1,200 but advised me that due to my status as a journalist I could probably have gotten by for half that amount.

Before Gallagher arrived I had done a story about some foreign students, perhaps as many as 80, receiving, as I put it, "revolutionary training ... at a special institute tucked away in the hills of Pinar del Rio province." Looking back, it was not a story I should have been too proud of. The story suggested that the Castro government was training students to stage armed revolutions in their homelands. This may have been so. But I had no proof, and, in fact, I had included a disclaimer in my story from a French student whom I quoted: "We are studying the Cuban Revolution and working to help the peasants." But the story also had implied they were learning guerrilla tactics. It was the kind of news from Cuba that I imagine Castro especially disliked but probably expected when done by a *Yanqui* reporter.

The story was published in the United States just about the time Gallagher must have been boarding the journalists' bus along with me to travel to the interior of Cuba to hear Castro make his annual 26th of July speech in the provincial capital of Santa Clara. Nobody from the government said anything to me about that story. I was thankful, but I would have been naive to presume they had missed it.

Castro's speech that day was instructional. He told Cubans what the government was trying to do to improve their lives, to arrive eventually at true, 100 percent communism. He decried capitalism but omitted his usual vitrolic attacks against the United States, noting only that the Moncada barracks attack 15 years earlier had begun the Cuban Revolution "right under the very nose of Yankee imperialism." Castro concentrated instead on Cuba's economic goals, explaining to people why they could not have all the food or clothing they wanted. He said equal income for everyone was one of the government's goals, eventually changing the meaning of money, which he called a capitalist "instrument of exploitation." He added that Cuba was "winning the battle of the economy and what is more important, this country is winning the battle of revolutionary conscience." He closed by praising "beloved comrade Ernesto Guervara" as the symbol of this conscience.

It was a relatively short speech for Castro, but the ride back to Havana still was 175 miles so the journalists' bus had to make an overnight stop where the hard times met us face to face. Gallagher and I shared a hotel room where the bathroom floor was flooded with water. There was only juice (no water) for breakfast, and the air conditioning hadn't worked for months. It was luxury compared to what he had seen in Vietnam, and certainly there was no danger of getting shot, but it gave Gallagher another look at how the folks in Cuba's hinterland were struggling. He went to bed reading, as I remember, a paperback spy novel.

In the morning he came up with some ideas for stories for me. I responded by telling him about a story I hadn't done. That story involved a Cuban who appeared in my office one day, upset and agitated. He said he was a relative of one of five Cubans sent illegally, he claimed, to work in the sugar harvest. He said all five were Cubans with U.S. passports who were awaiting their turn to leave the country. He added that his relative was in poor health and might not survive the hard work of cutting sugar cane with a machete. He gave me the names of the five. I suggested he go to the Swiss Embassy, the responsible outlet for handling U.S. interests in Cuba. He said he had tried that but had not been admitted because he was a Cuban. So I went to the Swiss Embassy, principally to try to confirm the five were in fact legal Americans. An embassy official took the names but seemed uninterested, outwardly pleased to inform me it might take weeks to get an answer.

I decided to try the *Granma*. Captain Jorge Enrique Mendoza, the editor of the paper and a longtime cohort of

Castro received me without delay. He listened to the story and thanked me for coming to his office but gave no hint he would do anything about it. Less than a week later, the Cuban man whose relative had been sent to cut cane returned to my office and said all five had been "rescued" from the sugar harvest and were safely back at home. I told him the editor of *Granma* probably was responsible for their return, but he ignored that idea, preferring to believe it was the customary American intervention of times gone by. He thanked me profusely.

After hearing my account, Gallagher said, "Don't get in the middle of something like that. Do the story. That's all." His words signified more than a mild reprimand: They reflected a concern born in the 1960s about a new kind of journalism that preferred subjectivity to objectivity. Proponents often called it "new journalism."

After more than a week in Havana, when Gallagher's departure was delayed by problems at Cubana de Aviacion, he left for Mexico and New York. With him he took plans to send new communications equipment and air conditioners to the AP office. He left behind words of encouragement for the AP Cuban staff and all his spare clothes.

Chapter Thirteen

HIJACKING ETC.

A giant poster of Che Guevara's face covering the front of
Sears, one of Havana's many empty stores, had begun to
fade. Everything in Cuba but salt was rationed. Life was hard
for everybody. Yet by my imperfect count, hijackers still
brought an average of three planes a month to Jose Marti
International Airport.

A lot of people who hijacked planes to Cuba were
misinformed or uninformed about their destination. At least
that was my assessment, which was backed up one day by a
Black Panther who walked into my office in Havana and
asked for help, something I felt sure he never would have
done in the United States. He had to be upset to do so, and
he was.

First, he gave me a name, not his Black Panther name,
and said he was a Panther party member and that he had
hijacked a plane to Cuba a few weeks earlier. I asked him to
wait a minute and started my tape recorder. I mentally
recalled a skyjacking that would fit that time frame and the
description of the hijacker by the plane's crew after they and
the hijacked passengers had returned safely to the United

States. His description had come on the AP news wire dateline Miami.

My visitor knew what he said was being recorded. He looked directly at the tape recorder and began by saying he was concerned because he had lost contact with other Black Panthers who had come to Cuba. He said he feared they might have been imprisoned, or, as he put it, "been made to disappear." I told him it was more likely they had been sent to work in agriculture, perhaps to cut sugar cane. He acknowledged that possibility but said there were other problems. The government, he said, would not allow "brothers" to make public statements. Officials had also suggested they get rid of their Afro hairstyles. And food, he said, was as meager as his social life. In short, he had not received the welcome he expected. He said he hoped that by speaking out to the U.S. press in Cuba that his unsatisfactory situation could be made known to Black Panthers back home. I was the only American press in Cuba he knew about.

I did not tell him that non-hijacking Black Panthers invited to Cuba and who arrived via Third World countries had been welcomed by the government and allowed to speak freely to the Cuban press. In fact, two of them, George Mason Murray, identified by the *Granma* as the education minister of the Black Panther Party, and Joudon Ford, New York leader of the Panthers, had held a news conference in Havana. They were guests of the OSPAAAL, the Organization of Solidarity of the Peoples of Africa, Asia and Latin America, a Castro-organized entity that did not live up to its intentions. *Granma* quoted Murray as saying the Panthers had "vowed not to put down our guns or stop making Molotov cocktails until colonized Africans, Asians, and Latin Americans in the United States and throughout the world have become free." This seemed much stronger stuff than the hijacker sitting in my office had in mind when he said his efforts to speak out had been ignored. I advised him the Cuban government probably expected him to integrate into Cuban life, which meant working in agriculture or wherever needed without complaint. I also told him I would do a story on his concerns, wished him luck, and bade him goodbye.

Within minutes I discovered that the recorder had failed to operate properly. I hadn't recorded a word. I went to the small hotel where he told me he was housed, left him a note and waited. He called the next day and agreed to repeat the interview, but suggested we meet somewhere other than the AP office. Perhaps he was catching on that I was somewhat *persona non grata*. We met at a downtown park bench, where he repeated his story and I taped it with the recorder in plain view. Two men, from their appearance and clothing, especially the heavy shoes, either from the Soviet Union or one of the East Bloc countries watched from about 30 yards away. They followed the hijacker, not me as he left the park. They apparently knew where I would be going.

His story got out via Western Union without much delay because the next day I got a call from a California radio station asking if the Black Panthers were planning to revolt against Castro. It was a silly question, but I answered "no, not a chance." The station offered to pay me for talking to it but I refused, which I later regretted. It might have been interesting to see them try to get a dollar check into Cuba.

Most hijackers probably did find life in Cuba more difficult than they expected but eventually settled anonymously into Cuban society without public complaints. Not every hijack to the island was for political reasons. I knew of two cases where fathers involved in domestic disputes brought children with them to escape adverse legal action in the United States. One was a U.S. major, a Vietnam medal winner stationed at Fort Sam Houston, Texas. He flew a private plane to Cuba, bringing his son with him. For unexplained reasons, he received better treatment than most hijackers and was given a house in a Havana suburb, a car, a maid, and a job teaching at a government language school. Perhaps he had denounced U.S. intervention in Vietnam. That would have brought a good response from the Castro government. Whatever the situation, it remained his secret. He refused to be interviewed by me or anyone else. The other case involved a black man from Philadelphia who had brought his daughter with him when he hijacked a jet to Havana. The Cuban government allowed his wife to come to Havana and take the child back home.

For the most part, trying to cover a hijacking was an exercise in futility. Many of the hijacked planes came from Miami, meaning that traveling at 500 mph, they could cover the 150 or so air miles to Havana's Jose Marti airport before I could weave my way through perhaps 10 miles of Havana pedestrian and vehicle traffic on Ranco Boyeros Boulevard at 30 mph. Even if I was alerted to the hijack by a message or telephone call from the AP in New York in time to beat the hijacked jet to the airport, the chances of even seeing the hijacker were slim. The chances of talking to anybody on the hijacked plane were nil. Cuban airport security saw to that.

Only the Western press in Cuba seemed interested in covering hijackings, and UPI's man, being a Cuban who wanted to leave the country, did not concern himself with something he knew the government would not like. The correspondent for Agence France Presse, who always liked to please his hosts, suggested both AP and Britain's Reuters news agency should do like he did and quit covering hijacks. Such coverage, he contended, was largely useless and of course of little interest in France.

But Reuters correspondent James Pringle and I deferred. We worked out a system that was somewhat successful. Taking turns, one of us would boldly go in the main entrance to the airport, thus attracting most of the security. The other would go to an outside window of the Salon de Honor, where the hijackers usually were debriefed and questioned by Cuban security. Kneeling down, either Pringle or I could look under a gap in a curtain. Sometimes it paid off mildly. My big score from window peeking was being able to report a hijacker who had arrived carrying not a bomb or a gun, but a saxophone. Another time, at the excited urging of the New York foreign desk, I sped probably at 35 mph to the airport to cover the arrival of a hijacked plane with American comedian Flip Wilson on board. If he said anything funny in Havana, it remains unreported. I never saw him.

Some days were busier than others. I remember seeing a hijacked Pan American jet roll to a stop beside a hijacked Eastern airliner one weekend. One of the few officials at

Foreign Ministry Press section who enjoyed a little humor once remarked to me: "Hey, Wheeler, when are you going to hijack a plane to the United States. Why not, if it's a Cuban plane they won't prosecute you, either."

The Swiss Embassy representing U.S. interests said in late 1968 that so far none of the hijackers had contacted it for help. The majority settled into Cuban life. Some went on to other countries. In a few cases, the government gave the names of hijackers who asked for political asylum, and they were not heard about again. But Havana's policy leaned toward discouraging hijackings because of the delicate diplomatic and political problems they could produce. A crash or the death of a passenger on one of the jets could have brought a political crisis with the United States.

With each plane's turnaround at Havana's airport ,the Cuban government collected a landing charge estimated at $10,000, not a great amount, but badly needed hard currency for Cuba's hard times. And hard they were. Castro admitted this publicly several times in his speeches. But details and figures described the situation better. Nearly 10 years after the Cuban Revolution, a Havana family of four with a monthly income of $260 was spending 73 percent of its income on food. This compared with 46 percent in pre-Castro, unrationed Cuba, according to figures from the then defunct theoretical journal *Cuba Socialista*.

The lopsided figures on food spending, however, were somewhat misleading because there was little to buy except food, and many other expenses had been eliminated. Rent was free. So were medical services, education, weddings, funerals, public telephones (when they worked), sports, cultural events, and nursery care. There were virtually no income taxes and absolutely no need for lawyers. Government appointed officials and judges handled legal matters. Almost everything was rationed: bicycles, soap, beer, cigars, toilet paper, and food. A worker was entitled to two shirts a year and asked to forget overtime by working twelve hours for eight hours of pay. Men were urged to give office jobs to women and go to work in industry, agriculture, or construction. Students were expected to spend their vacations working in the fields.

Considering these hardships, it becomes clearer why Castro was so willing to trade Czechoslovakia's sovereignty for Soviet financial support in Cuba. But I didn't see it that way at the time. I was too busy looking at the long lines of Cubans trying to get enough to eat. Getting details on the daily food struggle required going into small shops and stores taken over under nationalization and run by Committees for the Defense of the Revolution members. One day a CDR militant followed me from a store back to my office and demanded to know what I was doing asking all those questions. For a moment I wanted to wag my forefinger at him and give him the words I heard so often — "companero los documentos, por favor" — and tell him he needed permission to enter AP premises, then perhaps order him out. But I didn't, and he departed after a handshake and an explanation that I was seeing how well nationalization was working.

Nearly 40 percent of the population in the late 1960s was less than 15 years old, and some of Cuba's youth in those hard times reacted to the nationalization with disgust and "unrevolutionary" behavior. In a speech Castro complained about juvenile prostitution, vandalism and delinquency and said some youths were tearing down posters of Che Guevara. A 19-year-old who told me he wanted to play American rock and roll music and live in the United States complained: "I can't talk with the Cuban government." An eighth-grade dropout said: "We don't have a word. We don't have money. We don't have a future." One complaint frequently whispered was that if you were not revolutionary, you could not get into Havana University, no matter how good your grades. Certainly it seemed to be an unofficial requirement, for on campus it was hard to find a student publicly against the government. Mayra Vilasis, a Havana University junior, was glad to talk. "What communism means to me is really dignity. Now I'm proud of being a Cuban. I wouldn't change my citizenship for anything."

Revolutionary feeling seemed extra strong on the Isle of Youth (ex-Isle of Pines) off Cuba's south coast. Along with about a dozen other invited journalists and diplomats, I visited the island in the fall of 1968. It was a guided and controlled tour. But I got a closeup look at the young people Castro hoped would embody Cuba's "new communist man." I talked to a 20-year-old mother putting in a 48-hour work week as a grapefruit packer. Her salary was the equivalent of $75 monthly. "I would work for nothing," she said. The *Granma* published a photo of me interviewing a citrus worker.

At the 13th of March Internadoan Elementary School, named after the date when Havana University students were slain trying to overthrow dictator Batista, there was plenty of emphasis on the Vietnam War. "This is the school of the future," a teacher said proudly as her students clapped and sang about killing "the Yankee assassins." A fourth-grader told me "the Americans are killing children in Vietnam." A fifth-grader declared "capitalism and imperialism are the enemies of all the peoples of the world. We are brothers of the Vietnamese."

All the grade-school students knew who Che Guevara was and the country where he had been killed, even if they were unable to locate Bolivia, New York, London, or Beijing, on a map. Cuban officials guiding the journalists through the school dismissed such educational shortcomings, saying if it weren't for the Revolution, many of the students would never have seen the inside of a classroom, let alone a map.

Had I had been consciously grading Cuban communism as an economic system at the time, I would have given it an "F." It did not meet communism's oft-stated utopian formula: from each according to his ability; to each according to his needs. There were still a lot of slackers in the cane fields on the Isle of Youth, in factories, and in the government. There was absenteeism from work. Castro had said so. The "moral incentives" once proposed by Che Guevara to replace "material incentives" were not working. So the ability part of the formula was clearly not being fully met.

However, Castro continued to try to pump up what he called the country's "revolutionary conscience." The needs part of the formula in Cuba was self-evident. Everyone in Cuba wanted and, to a certain extent, needed more material things than they were getting. Khrushchev's threat that communism would "bury" capitalism would never come true at the rate Cuba was going. I couldn't see how communism as an economic system could frighten anybody, and I was living in the middle of it. Why were Americans so worried?

Years later, as I looked at the massive poverty, corruption, lack of medical care, education, housing, and the great disparity between the wealthy and the poor in the rest of Latin America, I decided my judgment of Cuba's economic health was too simplistic. It deserved, even in its worst days, a "D" perhaps even a "C." Castro was "El Maximo Leader," and in the hard times he certainly was that, rated an "A" for effort. The rest of the country did not always match his fervor.

RED BEARD COWS
AND RABBITS

One quick result of the visit to Cuba by Associated Press boss Wes Gallagher was an assignment on his order for Ann to work as an AP photographer covering Castro speeches. To do this, Ann needed permission from the Cuban Foreign Ministry. Approval came, which surprised me. When Castro spoke, Ann, like other photographers, got about 30 seconds to shoot as many frames as she could, never getting nearer than 10 to 15 yards from the Cuban leader. This proximity to Cuba's leader brought Manuel Pineiro Losada, the head of Cuban intelligence into the security picture. Besides spy work, he had to know who was getting that physically close to his boss.

Called Barba Roja because of his flaming red hair and bushy red beard, Pineiro was considered one of the most powerful men in revolutionary Cuba, aside from Castro and his brother Raul. Barba Roja was respected and feared by those both for and against Castro, by people both in and outside of the government. He headed the Directorate General of Intelligence (DGI), a network that rivaled and often outsmarted both the KGB and CIA. His authority also allowed him to control activities carried out by the Directorate of State Security (DSI). Paco Teira testified to U.S. senators after he defected that although he had worked for the DSI and the Foreign Ministry, he also had to answer to the DGI and to Pineiro, often personally. Pineiro could poke his spyglass into almost anybody's business.

Besides being recognized for his red beard and his intelligence savvy, Pineiro also had a reputation as a womanizer. He was said to be especially attracted to American women, perhaps because his wife was an American former dancer. I had heard some of this via the Havana grapevine, although I was still surprised and concerned when Ann whispered to me one morning after a Castro speech that Pineiro had tried to get personal with her while she was shooting photos. She was frightened. So was I.

Then I had an idea. Later that day I asked her to come out on the terrace where I was certain no one could overhear us. I suggested we talk about Red Beard's attentions to her, but from inside the apartment where anyone with a listening device, meaning Pineiro's intelligence, could hear us. I wasn't at all certain the apartment was bugged, but we always acted as if it were. Although we had nothing to hide, we were careful what we said, even in the bedroom. Ann agreed my idea seemed worth a try. Perhaps it might embarrass Pineiro and make him drop his romantic endeavors.

Our brief skit for electronic listeners began in the living room. "Maybe Red Beard made a pass at you because you're an American and have red hair, too," I said. Ann said she didn't think that had anything to do with it. "I just wish he wouldn't do it," she said. Perhaps Pineiro had been trying to entrap her, I suggested as we walked in and out of the kitchen. "No he's just flirting, and it scares the hell out of me," she said. "I hope he quits it." As we passed into another room, I said, temporarily full of bluff and bravado, that I might have to bring the matter up at the Foreign Ministry if he didn't. Ann said she didn't want me to do that and repeated her hope that he would simply quit making passes at her. And at the next Castro speech he did.

Much later I learned that her assessment of Pineiro's actions had nothing to do with politics was probably 95 percent correct. Red Beard just liked to chase women. American journalist Georgie Anne Geyer, in her book *Buying the Night Flight,* wrote that Pineiro made personal advances on her almost immediately after she met him, and those moves continued until she left Cuba after a visit in 1966. She blamed her rebuffs of Pineiro's attentions for subsequent rejections of her attempts to return to Cuba after that.

In his testimony before the Senate Internal Security subcommittee in 1971, Teira indicated that Pineiro believed intelligence work allowed its people a certain amount of romantic license. He said Pineiro once became angry with him after Teira reported to the DSE that Osmany Cienfuegos, a Communist Party Central Committee member and brother of dead revolutionary hero Camilo Cienfuegos, had one too many drinks and made a pass at a woman at a reception. Teira said Pineiro told him "a man of my experience would know better than to report things like that because the girl was an enemy agent provocateur."

Pineiro's actions with regard to Ann, although they had ceased, revived a dormant paranoia I thought I had shed. This revival did not persist long, however, and I returned to what, for lack of a better description, I called my state of defensive awareness. I tried to develop Cold War calluses. This meant I suspected that I and anybody connected with me were being watched. But no matter. None of us was doing anything wrong that I was aware of. Nobody was being paid in dollars. Neither Ann nor I bought art that might be considered part of the Revolution's cultural heritage, nor did we take photographs that could be considered sensitive. We continued watching what we said in the apartment, office, restaurants, and almost everywhere else. If some Americans feared there was a communist under every bed in the United States, Castro suspected there was an American behind every plot to put him into one permanently. After the Pineiro incidents ended, I took it for granted that Castro remained suspicious of me and the AP, and what was reported.

Amidst the political chill for me in Havana there were pleasant surprises. A reception at the Czech ambassador's residence where Polish vodka greased the way for people to salute Prague and its "liberalization" by singing "Deep in the Heart of Texas." I had worked in Texas for 11 years, and Ann was Texan-born and reared, which I suppose explained part of that moment.

Revolutionary Cuba, however, did have a notable link with Texas — cattle. After Castro came to power, one of the U.S. holdings seized by the Cuban government was land and cattle belonging to the King Ranch in Texas, reportedly the world's biggest ranch, stretching from southern Texas to the Mexican border. The Texas cattle sent to Cuba by the ranch were Santa Gertrudis developed by the Robert J. Kleberg family that owned the giant Texas spread. They were a beef cow bred from Shorthorns and Brahmans to feed in pastures or whatever was growing in hot hostile climates.

The Santa Gertrudis breed was so successful that the King Ranch also set up livestock operations in the 1950s in Australia and Brazil, where the ranch worked with a Brazilian meat-packing plant. In Cuba, the Texans established a joint venture, combining the livestock business with a sugar company near Camaguey in the east central part of the island. Santa Gertrudis cattle, according to Tom Lea in his book "The King Ranch," flourished in Cuba.

Castro, however, was interested in producing milk, not beef, and had his own idea of how to do it after hours of home study and lots of reading. In his research, he may have come across the information that the King Ranch cross-breeding success was the result of the judgment by experienced practicing ranchers, not geneticists or people learned in animal husbandry, and he may have taken encouragement from this to try his own ideas. He was no rancher, true, but he was born in the country. More likely it was the same self-confidence that had convinced him that, because it was the right thing to do, he could carry out a successful revolution when the odds were heavily against him.

Whatever led him to his conclusions, he came up with the idea of cross-breeding milk-giving Holsteins with local zebus. The crossbreed, he said, was to be designated as the F-1 hybrid. Using semen of prize Holstein bulls and artificially inseminating the zebu cows, Castro predicted that by 1970 the island would have more than eight million milk cows producing four times as much milk per cow as before. This would be one answer to the nation's food problem.

Under his direction, the government quickly acquired several Holstein bulls from abroad. One prize bull from Canada named Black Velvet was touted to be able to inseminate 15,000 cows annually. An artificial insemination station center, one of a handful, was set up so Black Velvet could contribute his share. At 30-minute intervals during the bovine work day, the handsome bull would rush into a corral and mount a wooden stanchion covered with cow hide and designed to look like the rear end of a cow. The hide on the stanchion that Black Velvet mounted, incidentally, was reddish and looked very much like it came from a Santa Gertrudis. So did the cow hides that covered furniture in the visitors' waiting room. As the bull reached his climax, a worker would reach under the stanchion and catch Black Velvet's semen in a plastic tube. The day I watched this taurine display, I was joined by other visitors — schoolgirls who giggled, then cheered as they saw part of what Castro called the nation's economic development.

British embassy sources said visiting cattle experts repeatedly warned Castro the cattle cross-breeding idea wouldn't work, but their advice was ignored. Castro had decided earlier that agriculture, not just sugar production, was a key factor in Cuba's economic equation. In 1965 he said so by declaring it as the "Year of Agriculture." The F-1 hybrid plan was one result of that emphasis. The crossbreed eventually was able to produce four times as much milk as a typical Cuban cow, but the program never got off the ground. The British press reported in 2002 that Cuba still had a shortage of milk.

Another Castro plan to increase food production involved rabbits, an idea that apparently came from a new Havana restaurant that specialized in rabbit. The rabbit dinners were good, but the restaurant came no where near accommodating the number of Cubans who sought a square meal. Historically, Cubans favored chicken and pork, both non-existent for the average citizen. Obviously, it was easier to change people's politics than their eating habits. Rabbits were not the answer.

Economic problems invariably set off anti-Castro rumors in Cuba and abroad. One that I battled was from "Belgian radio," a rumor fountain by itself. Its reports on more than a couple of occasions caused me to drive by the only two places in Havana I knew of where Castro might be residing for the moment. This journalistic drill was not in fact one of those lighter moments. But it was how journalists in those days often tried to cover things in authoritarian, particularly communist countries.

In the Soviet Union journalists, along with other Kremlin watchers, traditionally reported who was present or not present in the reviewing stand at the annual Moscow May Day parades. In Cuba there was only one person whose presence or lack of it mattered. So when a cryptic and poorly-veiled message would come to me from the AP in New York saying something like "Belgian radio hears Castro under weather," or "Belgian radio has no Castro sighting for some time," I would have to drive by the Castro bunkers and see if there was any sign of turmoil before soldiers guarding the area motioned me away. The latter made things seem normal. So I took that to mean I could knock down the Belgian radio report. The often-cited journalistic dictum that says a minimum of three sources is required before confirming a report did not apply as far as I was concerned. If I had one reliable source I considered it a bonanza. Finally, I visited the Belgian ambassador and asked him if he was familiar with "Belgian radio." He said he wasn't. After a while, the radio rumors stopped.

People whose actions seemed to question the Revolution also ran into hard times in 1968. A crackdown began in the fall after Castro denounced saboteurs, parasites and loafers and told members of the CDR to be ever-vigilant against them. One target was a new generation, some of whose members the *Juventud Rebelde* said were acting like U.S. hippies. Young men who wore tight jeans (if they could find them), people with long hair, and young women in miniskirts were suspect. But there were others — talented people who the government said abused their positions.

The first criticism came from *Verde Olivo*, the armed forces magazine, where Defense Minister Raul Castro had great influence. It began a campaign to purge Cuban art and literature of undesirable foreign influences. One of the first and most notable targets was Herberto Padilla, a young poet who, at the beginning of the Cuban Revolution in 1959, had been a correspondent for the Cuban news agency Prensa Latina in the United States. But nine years later, Verde Olivo suggested he had violated Castro's rule on artistic freedom: "Within the Revolution, everything; outside the revolution, nothing." This could have been stated more quickly and bluntly as, "If you aren't with us you're against us."

The ideological discord between writers and communist party militants came to the forefront after Padilla won that year's poetry award from UNEAC, the Union of Cuban Writers and Artists that Castro had originated. Padilla went under attack, specifically for a poem called "Outside the Game." He had dedicated it to a Greek communist poet imprisoned by the Greek military government in 1967, but its sentiments seemed also to reflect Padilla's incipient beliefs. Officially, he was criticized for being ambiguous. One non-Cuban translation of the poem in part said: "The poet! Kick him out! He has no business here. He's out of bounds." Of course it is doubtful if this ambiguity or hidden message, if that's what it was, reached the peasant sweating and swinging a machete or the worker doing an overtime stint without pay. But it upset the ideologues in the Cuban Communist Party. And there were unconfirmed rumors that the government crackdown on the artistic community came partially at the behest of the armed forces, some of whose leaders were worried about reports of homosexuality among the intellectual and talented elite.

Then there was UMAP, an acronym for militarily-run forced labor camps. Homosexuals and suspected homosexuals were reportedly being sent there by the dozens. While homosexuality was unofficially taboo, it was seldom mentioned publicly in those days. But it was considered clearly outside the Cuban Revolution. Padilla, of course, made himself unavailable to the foreign press while I was there. He may not have disliked the foreign press as much as Castro, but he undoubtedly knew that talking to a foreign correspondent could only cause him new troubles. The Verde Olivo attack itself presaged trouble. He was arrested and held briefly in 1971. Disgraced, he eventually left Cuba for the United States 10 years later.

Chapter Fifteen

10 YEARS, 10 MILLION?

Fidel Castro celebrated his 10th anniversary as head of the Cuban government, maker of the Cuban Revolution, and the most talked about Latin American since Simon Bolivar with a speech. There was nothing too special about that. He has been estimated to have given at least 2,000, maybe as many as 3,000 speeches. Not all of those speeches were recorded or made in public.

But the tenth anniversary was something special, proof to the "Yankee imperialists" to the north who kept hoping for his downfall that Castro and his Revolution could endure. It was also a new call to arms and machetes for the tens of thousands of Cubans who massed in Havana's Plaza de la Revolucion on January 2 to hear Castro declare that 1969 from that moment on would be known as the "Year of Decisive Endeavor."

Like many communist slogans of those times, it was a mouthful if you planned on chanting it at a rally or using it in everyday conversation. But everyone in the plaza who heard the Cuban leader, or saw him on television, or listened to him on the radio, knew it meant more hard work and sacrifice in order to reach Castro's frequently announced goal of 10 million tons of sugar production the next year. Nineteen sixty-nine was to be a rehearsal for 1970. In fact, Castro said the year would really be eighteen months long to include the sugar harvest of 1970. There would be no yuletide or New Year's celebrations until July of 1970. The government had already dropped military parades on Labor Day, May 1, and from other anniversary celebrations because armored vehicles, especially tanks, gobbled up too much precious gasoline.

The capitalist record was 7.2 million tons, reached in 1952. But sugar production in the 1968 harvest had been estimated at just over 5 million tons. The low yield was blamed on a drought. Castro said the 10 million ton-goal in 1970 would be reached "with or without drought." To do this, the government began preparing the biggest labor mobilization in the island's history. It spent an estimated $200 million to improve refineries, spent thousands of man-hours planting and fertilizing new cane, building dams and irrigation lines, and schooling technicians. I quoted a Western diplomat as saying he believed the goal would be met because "Castro has committed himself too deeply not to succeed. " But he added what many Westerners suspected might happen: "After all," he said, "this is a communist government. It can sacrifice 1969 for 1970."

The government had given no sign of that, however, as it continued giving detailed plans. It said that in 1970 it would harvest one million more acres of cane, a total of 3.6 million acres. The country's 152 sugar mills were estimated to have a grinding capacity of about 7.5 to 8 million tons, but the Sugar Mininstry said that capacity would be upped by 2.5 million tons by 1970. On paper, the plans looked good, although United Nations figures showed that Castro had never approached the yield per acre of pre-Castro days. The government said it had built a cane-cutting force around a nucleus of 75,000 permanent cane cutters. But it said for 1970, even with increased mechanization, it planned to put 400,000 cutters in the field. Castro exuded both confidence and enthusiasm as he briefed Cubans on the work ahead. He had been planning for the 10 million tons since 1963, when he first announced the goal.

The "Year of Decisive Endeavor" was just a start on the country's agricultural development, an effort that would grow by 15 percent a year Castro promised his audience. In the meantime, family sugar rations would have to be cut to six pounds a month, a move, he said, that would save the nation $10 million in foreign exchange. It was unspoken but clearly evident to me that even mild criticism of the "decisive endeavor" in which the nation was about to embark upon would not be treated lightly, especially if it came from foreigners. Anything that could be interpreted as skepticism was going to be risky. Castro had bet the limit with his 10 million tons, and I had to report how it played out.

First, however, I did a review of 10 years of Cuban Revolution. Since Castro had been in power, he and his Cuban followers had snuffed out a small anti-Castroite guerrilla movement, formed a communist alliance with the Soviet Union, defeated the U.S.-backed invasion attempt at the Bay of Pigs, gone unhappily through the 1962 missile crisis, and survived the U.S. economic blockade. Castro had also avoided at least half a dozen U.S. assassination attempts.

But the Revolution had not been without dissent. After 10 years, anti-Castroites, although officially muffled, were still around. Their exact numbers were not known. Certainly they represented only a minority. Some claimed their ranks had grown with Cuba's economic hard times, but I had encountered only a few. Almost all of them would have settled for leaving the island. Bitter and frustrated, they saw only worse years ahead for themselves.

Pro-Castroites, easily the overwhelming majority, acknowledged the Revolution still had a long way to go in 1969 but contended that the revolutionary government was a success. For many Cubans, the fact that the government had survived for a decade was evidence enough that the Revolution was working and would get better.

Figures I got from Western embassies in Havana, United Nations reports and the Cuban government showed deep changes in 10 years in Cuba. Those changes also showed the results had produced neither the shining example Castro backers desired nor the widespread threat to the hemisphere that his detractors feared. I tried to add it all up and get a total. In education, Castro's government had cut the illiteracy rate by 90 percent. True, some Cubans, especially the elderly in remote areas could do well just to write their names. But young people were no longer illiterate. An estimated 150,000 were government scholars. Per capita expenditure for education had risen 400 percent.

The government had increased the number of hospitals and clinics from 44 in 1959 to 177 by 1967 and set up more than 200 health centers, where there were none before. The emphasis was on getting medical service to rural, remote parts of the island. The number of doctors in Cuba increased from 6,300 to 7,000. New medical graduates were required to serve two years in rural areas. The government said the infant mortality rate was reduced, and there had been no indigenous malaria cases since June of 1967.

Progress in housing was not so good. The government had put up hundreds of prefab housing units across the country but not nearly enough. Too many peasants still lived in thatched bohios. In urban areas the housing shortage was acute. Apartments were overcrowded and utility service undependable. A big housing project on the outskirts of Havana remained unfinished, apparently for lack of materials. Many lavish houses left by wealthy Cubans emigrating to the United States to escape the Castro government had been turned over to scholarship students and by 1969 were badly in need of maintenance, like much of Havana. But some of the capital's slums were slowly disappearing. This would have been a giant stride almost anywhere else in Latin America.

The Revolution claimed it had done comparatively well in the arts, although Western diplomats liked to forecast that Castro's hard revolutionary line was wiping out a generation of intellectuals and creativity. The government had established the Casa de Las Americas, a house of culture headed by Castro's longtime friend and 26th of July pioneer, Haydee Santamaria. Castro had pushed to set up the Union of Cuban Writers and Artists. He had ended Havana's claim to being the "blue movie" capital of the world with the Cuban

Institute of Cinema Art. In 10 years it had produced 44 films, 204 documentaries, 94 technical films, 49 animated cartoons, and 435 newsreels, in one of which (the 1967 OLAS meeting) I had rated a brief reference as the "magnifico muchacho."

All of the films had a propaganda, but some less than others. "Memories of Underdevelopment," a film version of writer Edmundo Desnoes' book about a bourgeois Cuban who had trouble finding his place in the Revolution left some viewers wondering if Desnoes had found the answer. Many documentaries were instructive and educational but with a theme. The *Granma* bluntly defined the rules: "It cannot be forgotten that every shot, every sequence, every short subject, every documentary, every newsreel has but a single theme: the Cuban Revolution."

After 10 years, Castro was still denouncing Cubans who wanted to go to the United States. In private he was said to become incensed, particularly when badly needed professional people and technicians wanted to leave the Revolution and the island. Since January 2, 1959, when he took over, an estimated 5.5 percent of the country's 8 million people had left Cuba. About 4,000 were departing monthly in 1969, most of them on special government-approved flights to the United States from the beach resort of Varadero. Some were going to Spain, where they would await U.S. permission to enter the United States.

The emigration was a relief valve for dissidence. It got rid of a few plotters, a few anti-government activists. But for the most part, the emigrants (Castro called them gusanosor worms) were simply people who wanted no more of the

Castro Revolution. In order to leave, they had to leave behind all their property, including wedding rings. Doctors could not go until they had helped train a physician to take their place. Despite the rigid requirements, the nosey surveillance by their neighbors, and the government's disdain, thousands were reported on waiting lists at the Swiss embassy in Havana. The embassy declined to say how many names it had, but a Cuban who claimed to have seen most of the lists at the embassy told me the number ran past 190,000.

Those whose day of departure finally came were taken by bus from Havana to the Varadero airport, an arrival spot for tourists going to the beach resort area east of Havana in the pre-Castro days. I was allowed to watch one of the flights depart but was prevented from speaking directly to the passengers by my Foreign Ministry escort. It is doubtful if any of them would have said anything at that time anyway. Most of them looked as if they feared something would happen at the last second to prevent their leaving. It was strangely quiet in the departure lounge. The few children among the group were repeatedly hushed and hugged by their parents. In 20 minutes or so the U.S. chartered DC-8 would have all of them in Miami.

It also is doubtful if they had glimpsed or even thought about one of the last great vestiges of pre-Castro capitalism — the nearby 450-acre du Pont estate that had been taken over by the government. They didn't look like the kind of Cubans who would have been invited there. The property was acquired by the head of E. I. du Pont de Nemours and Co. Inc., Irenee du Pont, who had decreed the estate and its

20-room mansion "a stately pleasure dome" and named it Xanadu, taking a clue from Samuel Coleridge's famous poem (and Orson Welles' film "Citizen Kane"). Du Pont had hoped it would help some of his rich friends to join him in developing the resort area. The Castro government had turned part of the mansion into a restaurant after du Pont died in 1963. The head of du Pont's staff of servants for 31 years, Carlos Diez, was still employed as a manager of sorts at the restaurant by the Cuban government at the same salary du Pont had given him, $300 a month. Meals were expensive and restricted to foreigners.

As the 10th year of revolution got underway, the militant Committees for the Defense of the Revolution stepped up vigilance against vandalism and reported outbreaks of arson and sabotage. "The most important work of the Committees for the Defense of the Revolution is revolutionary vigilance," Luis Gonzalez Maturelos, the CDR national commander, reminded its 2.5 million members. Night patrols began.

I wrote a story about how Cubans were trying to cope with a shortage of cigars and cigarettes. The choice for smokers was either two packs of cigarettes or two cigars a week. In 1966 the government had centralized the tobacco industry under a new organization called Cubatobaco. Before that centralization, the country had reported an excess of 79 million cigars. The government had given no explanation for the current shortage. Surely Castro, who at that time was still smoking cigars, wondered what had caused the problem.

Other things happened after 10 years as well. I wrote a letter to Major Sergio de Valle, the minister of the Interior, saying I had received an unsolicited copy of a letter written by a political prisoner who accused Cuban authorities of "torture, assassination, and general abuse of prisoners." I asked to talk to him about the accusations. My letter was never acknowledged, and no story came of it.

Months earlier, a senora in her 60s shuffled through my office door one day to beg me to do something about her son, who was on a hunger strike in prison. She said he was protesting that he and others like him who were political prisoners needed to be treated as such, not like the ordinary criminals with whom they shared space. It was the kind of stance Castro tried to achieve and did to an extent when he was a prisoner of Batista. I telephoned the Interior Ministry to ask for an interview on the matter. That request was also never acknowledged, but within a week the senora was back in my office to tell me her son had been hospitalized and was being fed. She fell to her knees to thank me and wept. Stanley Graham, who had undoubtedly heard her story, came in from the teletype room and helped me get her to her feet while I tried to explain I had nothing to do with her son ending his hunger strike.

The number of political prisoners in Cuba during my time was estimated variously at less than 10,000, less than 15,000, and by Castro himself in talking to journalist Lee Lockwood at "about 20,000." None of those figures was official. I could never get any of them independently confirmed.

Castro did have a rehabilitation program that allowed people imprisoned for political crimes to leave prison if they promised not to stage counterrevolutionary actions and if they met certain other conditions. I never got any figures on how many did. But the program probably kept the number in prison in flux. There was no Amnesty International, the London-based human rights organization, in Cuba at that time. Twenty-five years later, Amnesty was to report the number of political prisoners, including new detainees, as being in the hundreds, not the thousands. I never wrote a story on political prisoners because I never had anything I considered factual enough.

Castro, I reported in April, had said the 1969 zafra harvest was not going well. Non-government reports said it might make only 5 million tons. The Cuban leader said bad organization was partly to blame for the year's poor sugar yields. He noted other problems. Many administrators of state work centers had no more than a sixth-grade education, he said. "In many of these cases, they are bright persons, intelligent persons, very gifted persons, but this unfortunately is not enough." He said other agricultural projects besides the sugar harvest were suffering. "Our cadres, our party, will have to learn how to wage and win simultaneous battles," he said. His assessments were not exactly fresh news to anyone living on the island.

Western economic reports had been saying many of the same things since nationalization had thrown the country into a bureaucratic muddle. Cubans from Santiago to Pinar del Río sensed if they didn't know outright that the country's agricultural revolution still was a long way from being achieved. The daily shortages of food, clothing, medicine, and gasoline, as well as the extra work hours showed them that. But the emphasis was already on next year. Posters proclaiming "the 10 million are coming" dotted the countryside. A big neon sign flashed the same news in red, white, and blue on Havana's main streets. More than 110,000 volunteers, mostly young people, were reported working in the hot, Texas-like Camaguey province. High school students who normally spent 45 days in agricultural work were enlisted to do double that time. Workers in westernmost Pinal del Rio province pledged to work twelve hours daily. Plans were made to bring young Americans to Cuba next year to cut cane. They would work in special "Venceremos" brigades taking that name from the words Castro used to close his speeches — Patria or Muerte Venceremos — "Fatherland or Death, We Will Win."

On the Isle of Youth foreign students were already working in agriculture with members of the Union of Young Communists (UJC). I met a young French Canadian socialist who was married to a Cuban and who had been working on the island because he wanted to help the Revolution. He told me that the young workers often fudged on the number of holes they had dug to plant citrus trees and that several of the UJC leaders abused their authority to gain special sexual favors. He said he was "disillusioned," tired of working for 70 pesos ($70) a month, and fed up with political instruction that consisted largely of listening to a UJC leader read old Castro and Che Guevara speeches. He said he was going home. But he was only one voice among hundreds, and he was not a Cuban. Again, I decided against doing a story.

In May, as the rainy season approached, the planting of cane for the next year's 10 million tons was reported behind schedule. I wrote it down for the future.

About this time Ann left for the United States to speak to the Associated Press meeting of its subscribing editors. AP President Gallagher had been impressed with her ability, grit, and good sense during his visit to Cuba in mid-1968 and had decided this time the wife of a foreign correspondent rather than the correspondent should address the editors at their annual meeting in New York. She did and impressed them so much they asked that her speech about day-to-day living in Havana be storified as a special AP feature for Sunday newspapers. It was and got wide usage, what the AP called good play, probably better than anything I ever wrote. The Voice of America (VOA) also liked it. Without AP knowledge or permission, it translated her speech-story into Spanish and had a female member of the VOA broadcast it on the frequency to Cuba. It was heard clearly all across Cuba and not liked by anybody who liked Castro.

But the government said nothing publicly and reserved its anger for me. The Foreign Ministry let me know about it the minute I returned with Ann from the United States via Spain. The government apparently had not been angry enough, however, to refuse our reentry. But the atmosphere around me quickly became noticeably cooler. It was not just confined to officialdom. One indication came from an artist friend, Cesar. We had socialized with him and his wife in the past. Without a hint as to why, he suddenly became distant. Finally, he asked that I not contact him in the future.

The VOA incident also soured one of my few jokes, which went like this: Castro used to like to get in a jeep and ride out in the country unannounced to talk to people, most often peasants. That part of the joke is true. The rest is not. One day he and his jeep came upon a small boy, scuffling along a dusty road. Castro asked the boy if he would like a ride to his home and the boy replied: "My mother told me not to accept rides from strangers." Puzzled, Castro said "but my son, surely you must know me. I am on TV all the time." The boy replied, "We don't have a TV." Then Castro added: "But I am also on the radio." Whereupon the boy raced down the road and ran to his hut, where he grabbed his mother's skirt and cried: "Mama, mama I just met the Voice of America."

A little levity in Cuba was becoming more welcome by the day, and although I seldom pass on jokes, I used one when I wrote about what I described as "a small war of rumor and humor between pro-Castro and anti-Castro Cubans." The joke, to my thinking, was rather dull, but it was a welcome diversion from news about the 10 million tons. It showed up about a week after the United States landed men on the moon on July 20, 1969. On that day, AP New York messaged me and wanted to know if Castro had been watching television and what the Cuban government's reaction had been. Television sets in Havana normally could not pick up television signals from the United States, but if the atmospherics were just right, sometimes there was reception for a few minutes. Once by chance I saw three plays of a New York Giants football game before everything from Miami television faded away.

I often thought if Cubans could see some of the TV commercials from the United States offering soap, clothes, beans, rice, nylons, or used cars for only $50 down and a like-monthly payment, they would probably become even more fully resentful of Castro's hardship rules. There was, however, virtually no chance Cubans had seen the moon landing on U.S. television. But Castro had access to special equipment, and he might have seen the landing. I knew Castro was a longtime baseball fan and also wondered if he was watching the New York Mets in the year they would eventually win a World Series. So I asked if Castro had seen the moon landing, and they said without detail that he knew about it. The joke then went like this: President Richard Nixon cabled Fidel Castro after the Apollo 11 landing: "We have put two men on the moon." Castro looked out at the sugar cane fields and wired back: "That's nothing. We have put a million people in the sun."

A little over a week after the moon landing, I was walking with about 100 other people, none of them from the government, at the funeral of former Cuban President Ramon Grau San Martin. In his student days, Castro had disliked Grau immensely. He felt Grau had deceived the Cuban people by allowing corruption, graft, and mismanagment during his 1944-48 term. Grau was one of the inept "musical chairs" presidents accused by Castro of enriching themselves and their friends while keeping Cuba under the thumb of the United States. Grau's type of rule had led Castro into politics. This was all before my time.

I attended Grau's funeral not as a mourner, and certainly not as an admirer, but as a reporter to write that the ceremony was one of the government's free funerals and that the old Cadillac that carried Grau to his grave was supplied gratis. "A president under capitalism was treated as an ordinary citizen under communism," I wrote. It was what was to be expected in an egalitarian society. Not startling news, but a story I had seen and could write.

About this time Telesforo Diaz, the latest head of the foreign press section of Cuban Foreign Ministry, and his aides called me in to ask that I use my "influence" with the U.S. State Department on behalf of the Cuban news agency Prensa Latina. They said the State Department had notified Prensa Latina that its budget for operating (covering the United Nations mostly) in New York City in the future would be limited to around $5,000 yearly, a ridiculously low figure. They also pointed out that I was free to go anywhere in Cuba, while Prensa Latina correspondents were restricted to traveling no more than 25 miles outside of the New York metropolitan area. The ministry was correct about me having no travel limitations, even with gasoline rationing. But several months earlier I had canceled a trip to Pinar del Rio province because, after I had advised the ministry where I planned to go, it had suddenly assigned a ministry escort to go with me. Orwellian bureaucracy then lightened the moment. When I tried to cancel my hotel reservation for the trip, I was told I could not do so until it had been confirmed.

As for Diaz and his party, I told them I had no influence whatsoever with the State Department or any other branch of the U.S. government. I told them the best I could do would be to pass on their complaint to the AP in New York. I did so with an uneasy feeling that I could end up in the middle of a fuss that was beginning to sound a lot like the tit-for-tat exchanges of the Cold War that often got correspondents thrown out of Moscow and Washington. Was Havana next? I put aside worrying about the answer.

For several months I had been receiving copies of provincial newspapers after I requested them from the Foreign Ministry. I had asked that I be allowed to pay for the newspapers, but the government refused my offer, saying the Revolution did not charge for such things. The newspapers were free and informative. My favorite was *Adelante* (Forward or Onward in English) from Camaguey, a key province in sugar cane production in the middle of Cuba and a major target in the government's mobilization of manpower to reach the 10 million tons. When there was a shakeup in the local communist hierarchy the newspaper said so. If there were Camaguey problems, they were usually reported.

The *Adelante* also reported "good news" but it was not required as was the *Granma* to print all the texts of Castro's speeches. It couldn't afford or obtain the newsprint for such a venture anyway. One issue of the newspaper had some startlingly frank figures. The paper reported a massive effort by workers but said they had not planted enough sugar cane in 1969 to reach the province's goal in the drive for 10 million tons in 1970. Without Camaguey making its quota and even discounting reports of labor refinery and transportation problems elsewhere, there was little chance the goal of 10 million tons would be reached. I sent a story saying that. A similar report was written by the correspondent of the Czech news agency, CTK, a Prague

Spring advocate barely hanging on in Havana. We had something else in common. Unknowingly, we were both in trouble.

Castro fired back at any doubters. On July 14, 1969, he spoke at a rally inaugurating the 1970 sugar harvest and gave Cubans this hope for the future. "In 1980 we should have twice as much cane as in 1970," he said. "We shall have an absolute abundance of food; all the rice, all the milk, all the food that we need in the necessary amounts. We shall have more clothing, we shall have more shoes, we shall have more communications, the services will continue improving. And in the next decade there will be no years like this."

Chapter Sixteen

JUDGMENT DAY

A judge can't be a journalist. But a journalist can be a judge and often is. I proved that on September 6, 1969, just shy of 25 months after Fidel Castro had publicly raked me over the coals for saying I was a journalist not a judge.

In fact, during those months I had probably been making judgments on most stories I wrote about Cuba. I am sure I thought such judgments had been arrived at fairly and with reasonable objectivity. After all, not everything the government said was news or always true. Even then it didn't say much, except for the words that came out of Castro's mouth.

On September 5, a Friday, the Cuban government announced it had caught a Mexican diplomat spying for the United States. It identified him as Humberto Carrillo Colon, the press counsel at the Mexican Embassy in Havana, a man I knew professionally but only barely socially. Specifically, the government said Carrillo was spying for the U.S. Central Intelligence Agency. It demanded that he be turned over to the Castro government for trial.

The accusation became public when it was published in the *Granma* two days after Havana had sent a formal note to the Mexican government charging Carrillo with exchanging coded radio messages with the CIA somewhere in Florida, and in Nassau in the Bahamas.

Mexico diplomatically denied the charges. Mexican Ambassador Miguel Cobian Perez called the note "inadmissible," and said Carillo was in his custody, presumably at the embassy, and would be flown out of Havana on the next available flight. He declined to talk further to me or other reporters about the case. In Mexico City, Mexican Foreign Minister Antonio Carrillo Flores (no known relation to the Havana Carillo) called the Cuban accusation "unacceptable," but he said Carrillo would be recalled from his diplomatic post in Havana.

In breaking the story, *Granma* reported that Cuban Foreign Minister Raul Roa's note to the Mexican foreign minister said the Cuban government began hearing coded broadcasts from CIA locales in Florida and Nassau on April 7, 1968, about a month after Carrillo Colon arrived in Havana. The note said coded broadcasts going the other way from Havana to Nassau and Florida were traced to Carrillo's Havana residence. It added that the Mexican diplomat "procured information on the activities of leaders of the Cuban government, especially on our prime minister, Major Fidel Castro putting to use not only this information to penetrate confidential matters of our government but also eventually so that it could be used for attacks on the lives of these leaders." Carrillo also was accused of using diplomatic correspondence normally inviolate to pass information to the CIA.

The *Granma's* news story went on to say that the Cuban Foreign Ministry note also asked that the Mexican government renounce Carrillo's diplomatic immunity and that he be turned over to Cuban authorities to be tried for "grave crimes committed against our country." This was aggressive talk from Havana to Mexico, the only Latin American country to have diplomatic relations with Cuba, and I noted it in my story.

Carrillo also spied on his own embassy and his own ambassador, the Cuban note said, and added that Carrillo left Cuba for 15 days in 1968 to receive training as a "Mexico operative" and on his return from Mexico on Dec. 10 that year, he brought in modern radio equipment supplied by the CIA. Havana said all of Carrillo's spying activities were carried out "in compliance with instructions received from the CIA."

Two questions popped up immediately for me. The first concerned the CIA. With Richard Nixon now in the White House, was the intelligence agency still trying to kill Castro? The second question related to how the Cubans got into a diplomatic pouch or bag? I left the first question alone, but included the second one in a follow up story on *Granma's* report the next day. In Western Union cablese it said: "IT UNEXPLAINED HOWEVER HOW HAVANA COUNTER INTELLIGENCE AGENTS KNEW WHAT INSIDE MEXICOS DIPLOMATIC BAG GRAF." That seemed fair enough to me. How did they know? Diplomatic correspondence was supposed to be untouchable.

But in the next paragraph I wrote, also in cablese: "ANOTHER QUESTION LIKELY BE LEFT UNANSWERED WAS WHETHER IN FACT CARRILLO WAS WORKING FOR THE CIA STOP CUBANS SAID THEY HAVE QUOTE IRREFUTABLE UNQUOTE PROOF HE WAS GRAF." That paragraph clearly was subjective. The Cuban government had already answered "yes" to the question of whether Carrillo was a CIA spy. And the Mexican government, while saying the charges were "inadmissible," had neither confirmed nor denied whether they were true. Anyway, the Mexican government probably didn't know if, as the Cubans had alleged, Carrillo was spying on his own embassy. What I had written could amount to strike three by any Cuban umpire's count. That meant I could be out.

Perhaps I was percipient. For some reason I can't remember, I thought I should clip the story as it clattered off the AP Western Union machine. I eventually did clip those two paragraphs. I know now why I have saved them. They showed clearly I had made a judgment again questioning whether the Cubans had proof of a CIA plot to get Castro.

On Sunday *Granma* came out with more details on Carrillo's activities, including reports he had advised the CIA of seeing "mysterious" objects off Havana's shore, perhaps indicating some kind of secret Cuban military weapon or something equally nefarious. This nonsense brought back Castro's words at OLAS two years earlier, when he said it would be naive to think the CIA was a "perfect ... very intelligent organization." I thought that if the CIA had paid Carillo anything, and the agency certainly must have, the organization wasn't very intelligent at all.

Granma included other details more interesting: a list of numbers, radio frequencies Carrillo was said to have used in his transmissions between Havana and Nassau and between Havana and somewhere in Florida. Even on first glance they rang true. As I read *Granma*, I thought about the few times I had talked to Carrillo at diplomatic receptions or at the Mexican embassy and tried to remember any of our conversations. I recalled talking about the coffee plants Mexico was providing gratis for Havana's Green Belt, but no political conversations, and I doubted there were any. If Carrillo had heard about Castro's public chastisement of me before he came to Havana and mistakenly thought that we somehow could be on the same team, he never showed any indication of it.

Later that day, Eduardo Kuri, a newly arrived correspondent for the Mexican news agency, Amex, invited Ann and me to a beach house outside Havana for a swim. There he called me aside and told me Carrillo had used the same beach house and one time, by chance, when Kuri was there, he had seen a folded piece of paper with numbers like those published in *Granma* fall from Carrillo's swim trunks. I resolved on hearing that I would go back to the Mexican embassy early Monday morning and ask them about the list of numbers published in *Granma*. I expected I would get no reply and although it would end up as a fruitless effort at getting any confirmation from the embassy I would do an updated story reporting more Cuban evidence that Carrillo was a CIA spy. I never got the chance.

The telephone call from the Cuban Foreign Affairs Ministry came a little before 3 a.m. It was Telesforo Diaz. He said I was to be at the ministry at three o'clock. I had sensed several times in talking to him before that he had a strong dislike for me, and one of my first thoughts was that he had called at that hour just to be petty. I decided he meant 3 o'clock in the afternoon, rolled over, and went back to sleep. Sometime after 3:30 a.m. Diaz called again. I was awake this time, instantly, and I suspected something serious was in the offing. As I drove up to the ministry I could see all the lights were on in the press section. I saw no other correspondents' cars, and then I knew for certain what was up.

Diaz could barely restrain his joy as he told me I was being expelled by the government for writing what he called anti-Cuban news. He said I was to catch the plane to Mexico in two hours at 6 a.m. I asked him if I could initiate a call to my office in New York. He smiled, the first time I had ever seen him do so, and said nothing. There was nothing left for me to say but thanks and so long. The whole procedure had taken less than two minutes. My two years, seven-months, and almost twenty-six days in Cuba were over. My first feeling was not one of relief but of regret. I thought Castro had made a mistake, and I still think so. And I had lost my job in Cuba. It was September 8, 1969.

While Ann threw things into suitcases, I asked the telephone operator to put me through to the AP's number in New York. The call went through. That had never happened before. I told Harris Jackson on the foreign desk, one of the best editors I ever encountered, what was happening and why. Then I went to the AP office and scooped up what files I could. I took Saturday's Western Union copy of my story and clipped out the two paragraphs I felt had brought the government down on me. I looked around the rest of the office — at the radio teletype room, its equipment now chattering away with stories for the afternoon papers south of the Mexican border and the machines with fewer problems than before, thanks to a new rooftop aerial. I looked at the new wire photo equipment and at the blessed new air conditioners, more results of AP president and boss Wes Gallagher's visit a year earlier. I had managed to get Gallagher entry into Cuba, but couldn't get him or me a meeting with Castro.

The office improvements had been purchased in Canada and sent by the AP via Canada (I presumed) to circumvent Washington's economic blockade. There was nothing else I could take. No time to go through the photo file. I had never thought about the AP peso account in the National Bank of Cuba before and didn't now. On the way to the apartment I glanced at the new (1968) AP Volkswagen Variant station wagon in the underground garage beneath my building, another AP present via Canada to make the correspondent's life in Cuba easier. As I entered the apartment building I saw two members of the CDR watching me. Then I called the AP chauffeur, Esmond Grant. He was almost too frightened to drive us to the airport. A friend from the British Embassy, Christopher Skeate, and another friend, Dick Spier, the manager in Havana of the Dutch airline, KLM, drove along with us. They were stopped by security inside the airport terminal and waved a goodbye.

At the check-in counter, *Cubana de Aviacion* demanded $48, not pesos, for excess baggage. They finally accepted

Cuban pesos after I told them I hadn't had any dollars for two years and a Foreign Ministry official who had met me at the counter intevened. Ann and I were taken to a small security room, where we waited for about four hours because the flight was late in taking off. The security officials were polite and offered coffee, which Ann refused. She thought it might be doctored.

Carrillo was on the same plane, an obvious "cute" arrangement by the government to demonstrate it was throwing out the CIA spy and the *Yanqui* journalist at the same time. Carrillo boarded the plane after we did and was seated toward the front, protected by Cuban security and another Mexican diplomat. I never saw or heard of him again.

As Ann and I flew toward Mexico City, I wondered what else we had left behind. Damp swim suits. A record player. Some Czech dishware. A cat. And my Pentagon identification card. At last Castro could have his "proof," except it wasn't. As the Vietnam war escalated, Gallagher had decided all AP foreign correspondents should have a Pentagon identification card in case they were suddenly called on to go to Vietnam. I had deliberately dumped my card behind a heavy piece of furniture when I discovered it in my wallet as I went to apply for a Cuban driver's license the first week I was in Cuba. It stayed there, forgotten the entire time I was in Cuba. I doubt even if the government had known about the Pentagon ID card it would have made any difference. They knew after two and a half years I had nothing to do with the CIA. I was being expelled as an unwanted American journalist.

I also thought about when Paco Teira testified in Washington. He identified Del Rio as an intelligence agent. I suppose Diaz and Lazo were, too. Paco, without saying so before his Senate quizzers, also shed some light on how Carrillo may have been uncovered as a CIA agent. Carrillo's compatriot and supposed friend, Mexican journalist Marta Solis, with whom the diplomat had frequent contact, was identified by Paco as working for Cuban intelligence.

The issue of *Granma* the day I was expelled, which I did not see until sometime later, reported my expulsion on Page 4. The headline "A Yankee Correspondent Expelled" topped a one paragraph story from the Cuban news agency Prensa Latina: "Because of news stories unfounded, distorted, and frankly hostile to Cuba, John Fenton Wheeler, the correspondent of the North American news agency AP was expelled from the country today."

The next day the Cuban Foreign Ministry gave an expanded version:

In the morning of the 8th of the present month Mr. John Fenton Wheeler, the correspondent of the North American news agency AP, was expelled from our country.

The motives which led to this decision were news stories sent by this correspondent obfuscating and putting in doubt the facts reported by the Revolutionary Government of Cuba in relation to the agent of the CIA ...

This inadmissible and unacceptable behavior of Mr. Wheeler is nothing new; he began his groundless distorted and frankly hostile campaign against Cuba on his arrival in our country in February 1967.

There was, however, a part of the Cuban Foreign Ministry note that belied a conclusion that I had been expelled only because the government felt I had doubted CIA intervention. The note also declared that I had been considered an enemy almost from the day I landed in Havana and began a "hostile campaign against Cuba." Had my very first story been hostile? If so, why hadn't I been tossed out a lot earlier? No, I decided my other misdeed, beside being what the government considered an apologist for the CIA, was being an AP correspondent, one of those people who Castro had said distort the news when they "write daily." The fact that I would no longer be around to keep track of the government's drive for the 10 milllion tons of sugar production did not register with me at the time. It may not even have been a part of Castro's thinking. But if the harvest was going to fail, he certainly would not have wanted the AP to report that before he did.

In Mexico City I responded to Gallagher's request to telephone him in New York and confirm safe arrival on the flight from Havana. "Don't worry. We've been kicked out of better countries," the head of the AP told me. I don't think either he or I thought the AP's ouster from Cuba would last the nearly three decades that it has.

My expulsion rated three paragraphs on Page 9 of the *New York Times*, barely more space than *Granma* had given the story. In my native Midwest, however, it got the front page in the *Kansas City Star* and of course in my hometown of Abilene, Kansas.

EPILOGUE

The great Cuban sugar harvest of 1970 failed to reach its goal of 10 million tons. Fidel Castro took a good share of the blame, fired some officials, made a token offer to resign, and somehow kept his Revolution intact. In fact, Cuba's hardest times seemed to ease from then on, until the Soviet Union died in 1991.

In those years while Havana was still under Moscow's financial umbrella, Castro engineered a new Cuban constitution, arranged for a transition of power that can put his younger brother Raul in command some day, had Cubans vote in a rubber-stamp legislature and repeatedly won elections as an unopposed candidate for president. No one, including me, even thought about elections when I was there.

Castro has kept communism alive, if not overly healthy, after 48 years in power. But to do so he has had to make changes, to liberalize. Tourism has been revived to lure Europeans and both North and South Americans. Havana has moved to restore diplomatic relations with the rest of Latin America. It has tried to do more business with foreign companies. The dollar has become tradable for the first time since 1959. Relations with the Catholic Church were improved by a papal visit. Christmas is back. American professionals have played baseball in Havana, and the Cuban national team has played in the United States. Cuban players sprinkle the lineups of U.S. major league teams.

But non-diplomatic relations between Cuba and the United States have improved only slightly. Ten White House administrations have continued the economic boycott against Cuba.

Cold War nonsense lingers on in both Havana and Washington. Many of the politicians who helped sustain the two-way enmity in my time are gone. So are a few of Washington's hardliners and many of Miami's anti-Castro militants.

Still, the political chasm between Cuba and the United States that I felt decades ago sometimes seems almost as wide as ever. The United States continues to restrict Cuban correspondents to covering the United Nations in New York. They can only travel within 25 miles of Columbus Circle. The Associated Press has reopened an office in Havana, joining CNN in Cuba. There are hopes that more U.S. news organizations will eventually be allowed in by Castro. But there have been few encouraging signs Washington would reciprocate.

I remain little more than a Cold War memory and a journalist *persona non grata* in Havana. I have tried on four occasions to return to Cuba as a journalist and have yet to get a reply from either Havana or the Cuban interest section in Washington.

My only connection with the Cuban past came when Paco Teira read the chapter about him published in the *Columbia* (Mo.) *Tribune*. I met him in Florida, far from the exile community he avoids. He is married, a grandpa, cautious, but a buoyant and loyal friend.

INDEX

C

California, 17, 131
Canada, 38, 63, 81, 144, 173
Carmichael, Stokely, 11
Castro speech, 1, 39, 106, 140, 141
Castro, Raul (Fidel's brother), 48, 50, 84, 118, 139, 146, 177
Castro, Fidel, iv, vii, 1-6, 8-13, 23-25, 27-31, 33-37, 39, 40, 43-56, 59-63, 67-74, 77, 78, 82-92, 93-102, 104-109, 111-127, 130-132, 134-162, 165, 167-170, 172-174, 176-178
Castro government, 55, 56, 61, 70, 88, 112, 124, 132, 153, 156, 167
Castro's guerrilla war, 49, 56
CBS (Columbia Broadcast System), 63
Central Committee, 4, 95, 96, 110, 141
Central Highway, 37
Chibas, Eduardo "Eddy", 44
Chisholm Trail, 15, 17
CIA spy, 170, 171, 174
CIA assassination team, 3
CIA (Central Intelligence Agency), 2-4, 8, 10, 12, 13, 24, 27, 43-45, 50, 52, 53, 59, 60, 65, 70, 72, 140, 167-171, 174-176
Cienfuegos, Osmany, 11, 141
Cleveland, 111
CNN (Cable Network News), 178
Cold War, iv, 24, 38, 51, 53, 54, 75, 78, 80, 93, 102, 142, 164, 178
Colombia, Mo., 84, 110

Columbia (Mo.) *Tribune,* 179
Committees for the Defense of the Revolution (CDR), 6, 86, 87, 104, 105, 118, 135, 146, 156, 173
communism, vii, 5, 24, 52, 56, 73, 83, 102, 109-111, 117, 125, 136-138, 163, 177
Council of Ministers, 29
Cuba, iv, 3-6, 8, 12, 24, 25, 27-29, 31, 33, 34, 36-38, 40, 43, 45-50, 52, 53, 55, 56, 58-60, 62, 63, 65, 68, 69, 72-74, 76-87, 88-90, 93-105, 107-113, 115-117, 119, 120, 122-126, 129-135, 137-139, 141-143, 145, 148, 152-154, 157-164, 167, 169, 172-176, 178
Cuba's Revolution, 3, 90
Cuban security, 28, 39, 77, 133, 174
Cuban Communist Party, 6, 95, 97, 100, 104, 114, 147
Cuban exiles, 8, 53
Cuban Foreign Affairs Ministry, 4, 32, 35, 57, 67, 139, 163, 171, 175, 176
Cuban immigration and customs, 27
Cuban intelligence, 5, 55, 57, 61, 94, 104, 139, 175
Cuban television, 100, 103
Cubans, 1, 4, 5, 8, 12, 28, 35, 45, 50, 52, 68, 70, 77- 80, 83, 88, 94, 100, 104, 107-114, 117-120, 124-126, 135, 145, 149, 151-156, 158, 161, 162, 165, 169, 170, 177

military, 5, 20, 37, 45, 47-49, 72, 76, 78, 94, 98, 103, 107, 115, 147, 150, 170

Moncada army barracks, 48, 115, 123

Moscow, 40, 47, 52, 53, 73, 75, 80, 83, 84, 93, 95, 96, 103, 115, 116, 118, 123, 145, 164

N

National Institute of the Tourist Industry, 106

NBC (National Broadcasting Company), 64

New York Times, The, 31, 35, 68, 69, 101, 176

New York City, 25, 163

Nixon, Richard, 52, 162, 169

North Korea, 38, 95, 102

North Vietnamese, 11

Novosti (Soviet news agency), 93

nuclear warheads, 53

nuns, 109

O

October 1962 confrontation, 53

oil, 30, 52, 83, 84, 93, 116

Oliver, J. G. Oliver, 15

Organization of Latin American Solidarity (OLAS), 8, 10-12, 60, 61, 85, 94, 154, 170

Ortodoxo Party, 44

Oscar Lujones Gonzalez, 36, 119

OSPAAL, 11

Oswald, Lee Harvey, 24

P

Paco Teira, 62, 96, 140, 175, 179

passport, 27

Perez, Miguel Cobian, 168

Peron, Juan D. Peron, 51

Philby, Kim, 103

Platt Amendment, 46

Playboy magazine, 13, 62, 64

Portugal, 104

Prensa Latina, 13, 62, 146, 163, 175

priests, 109

Q-R

Quint, Bert, 63

Reflector, 15, 16, 22, 23

Republican, 15, 16, 21-23

Reuters, 13, 58, 62, 72, 133

revolution, 3, 5, 6, 8, 11, 12, 28, 35, 45-48, 51, 53, 67, 68, 70, 72-74, 76, 81, 83-88, 90-92, 94, 96-101, 104, 105, 107-110, 117, 118, 123-125, 134, 135, 137, 143, 146, 147, 149, 151-156, 158, 159, 164, 177

Rio, Del Rio, 36, 37, 124, 158, 159, 163, 175

S

San Diego Union, 112

Santiago, 24, 37, 48, 158

Senate Intelligence Committee, 52, 121

Sierra Maestra, 48, 51, 56, 68, 94, 111, 120

Sourwine, J. G., 64

Soviet Union, 10, 38, 46, 53, 57, 73, 75, 83, 85, 90, 93, 96, 98, 100, 116, 131, 145, 151, 177

Soviet propaganda, 95

Soviet communism, 52

Soviet Embassy, 5, 95

Spain, 29, 34, 38, 45, 51, 70, 80, 104, 109, 154, 160

Spanish-American War, 46

Sputnik, 94

Student Nonviolent Coordinating Committee, 98

sugar, 32, 34, 47, 48, 52, 84, 87, 89, 91, 92, 105-107, 118, 126, 127, 130, 143, 144, 150, 151, 158, 162, 164, 165, 176, 177

sugar cane, 32, 91, 126, 130, 162, 164

sugar harvest, 34, 91, 92, 118, 126, 127, 150, 158, 165, 177

Swiss Embassy, 79, 126, 134, 155

T

Tarabochia, Alfonso, 60

television, 1, 30, 33, 68, 72, 73, 98, 100, 103, 113, 149, 161, 162

Third World countries, 130

Times of London, 103

Topeka Capital, 23

Topeka, 21, 23

Tourist industry, 106

tourists, 31, 35, 46, 106, 155

Transportation Ministry, 101

Truman, Harry, 23

U

U.S. State Department, 27, 163

U.S. Navy, 5, 76

U.S. television, 98, 162

U.S. journalists, 27

U.S.S. Maine, 29, 45

Union of Cuban Writers and Artists, 147, 153

United Press International (UPI), 8, 40, 58, 67, 98

United States, iv, 5, 9-11, 19, 22, 24, 27, 29, 33-38, 45, 46, 51-53, 56-60, 63-65, 68, 70, 75-82, 94-98, 116-119, 121-125, 129-132, 134, 136, 142, 146, 148, 153, 154, 160-162, 167, 178

United Nations General Assembly, 52

United Nations, 2, 28, 52, 151, 152, 163, 178

University of Missouri, 23

V

Venezuela, 51, 85

Viet Cong, 11

Vietnam, 5, 11, 24, 33, 46, 75, 77, 78, 80, 98, 102, 103, 110, 115, 117, 119, 122, 126, 132, 137, 174

W-Y

Washington, iv, 3, 5, 35, 40, 46, 51, 53, 73, 78, 112, 121, 123, 164, 175, 178

Western press, 28, 133

Western Union, 31-33, 35, 38, 131, 169, 170, 172

Wheeler, John Fenton, iv, 6, 59, 175

Wheeler, Ann, 28, 30, 35-37, 81, 83, 88, 89, 94, 95, 139-142, 160, 171, 172, 174

Wheeler, C. W. "Red," 15-17, 21-23, 25

Wild Bill Hickok, 15

Witker, Kristi, 99

World War II, 5, 20, 22, 122

Yanqui, 2, 36, 43, 67, 104, 110, 125, 174

ABOUT THE AUTHOR

John Fenton Wheeler attended the University of Kansas, where in 1949 he won the Sigma Delta Chi journalism fraternity reporting award. He began his journalism career as a copy editor for the *Topeka Daily Capital*. Two years later he became news editor of the *Corpus Christi Times*.

In 1963, Wheeler won an Inter American Press Association scholarship to Chile. After returning to the United States a year later, he began working for the Associated Press in Columbus, Ohio. In 1965, he was transferred to AP's foreign desk in New York. Two years later he was assigned to cover Cuba, where he lived and reported for nearly three years. In 1969, Castro expelled him.

Wheeler then became chief of AP's bureau in Madrid, which covered the Iberian peninsula, Spain and Portugal. He covered the demise of the Franco and Salazar's dictatorships. Wheeler then became bureau chief in Lima, Peru, and covered the country's guerrilla war with the Shining Path insurgency. He retired from the AP in 1985 and joined the *Tulsa World* as a senior editor, where he worked until 1991. He retired to Columbia, Mo.

Wheeler has tried to return to Cuba as a journalist, but Cuban authorities have refused to let him back in the country.